heartlines

I Love You – I Think

Heartlines

heartlines

Jane Pitt

I Love You – I Think!

A Pan Original

First published 1989 by Pan Books Ltd,
Cavaye Place, London sw10 9pg
9 8 7 6 5 4 3 2 1
© Jane Pitt 1988
ISBN 0 330 30427 5
Printed and bound in Great Britain by
Richard Clay, Bungay, Suffolk

Chapter 1

The trouble with H and me is mostly H.

'H' stands for Harriet. Harriet Catherine Victoria Wyndham-Jones to be precise. Her mother was reading a lot of those historical romances while she was expecting so poor H got landed with that mouthful (the Wyndham-Jones is another story, but I'll get to it in a minute). Not that anybody ever calls her Harriet, or Catherine or Victoria. We wouldn't dare. She'd probably jump down our throats and carry out a quick tonsillectomy while she was there very, very painfully. She's like that.

She's also my best friend. Has been since the day she tied my hair to the back of a chair when we were in infant school and then threw lumps of Plasticine at me. I seem to remember I screamed a lot and she just danced round me laughing. Funny how you get to be best friends.

We live five streets away from each other in what is supposed to be one of Britain's most historic and beautiful towns. That's what the guide books say anyway.

For 'historic' read that people kept on invading it for no particularly good reason.

For 'beautiful', well if you enjoy getting your heels stuck in the cobbles and bumping into things at night because half the street lights have gone out again –

fair enough. Oh, and not to forget getting snowed-in in winter and blown to pieces in the March gales.

The Queen Mum sort of owns it. Well, she's a warden of it, whatever that means, and she walks about it occasionally opening things like the new sports centre while all the traffic in the High Street piles into itself and the tourists ooh and ah.

In the summer you get every language from Greek to Glaswegian. In the winter if the butcher even looks at you while he's taking your money you know you've made a major breakthrough – and we've got some very attractive butchers.

It's OK if you like boats and antique shops and art galleries, and I don't suppose I'd *really* want to live anywhere else, but it's hardly what you'd call a thriving metropolis – it doesn't even have a cinema. And at six o'clock it usually decides to go to bed early.

Which is more or less what started H off.

Some nutter in our educational establishment which tries to drive silly facts into even sillier idiots like me decided that if we all got the money together we could go off for a winter break and break our necks on some ski slope in Scotland. His way of getting rid of us I suppose, even if he is quite dishy for a PE instructor. Anyway, H put both our names down without telling me. Our folks put all their feet down, in this case six feet because H's Dad did a runner a couple of years ago with a petrol-pump attendant and hasn't been seen since. So H's is a one-parent family and proud of it. That's actually where the Wyndham-Jones comes in. Mrs H was a Wyndham and Mr H was a Jones, but she got so mad at him she joined the two together. Anyway, coming back to the feet. They all said, on one of those famous round-table conferences parents have when they should be doing something more sensible, 'If you can find the money then you can go, but don't expect us to pay for it'.

H flipped. I shrugged. Climbing up and down a lot of snow in the Cairngorms or wherever didn't seem to me the best way to spend ten days, but when she gets an idea in her head you sort of find yourself going along with it. You don't have much option. It's a bit like sleep-walking.

'We've got to *do* something,' she yelled, windmilling her arms around and frightening the seagulls. We were down at Strand Quay at the time watching the motorists getting puzzled by the stupid roundabout. 'We've got to find some cash *somehow*. Think of it, Jan! All those Scottish guys in kilts! All those ceilidhs and hoots-mon!'

I thought. Then inwardly shuddered.

'Haggis and chips, Aberdeen Angus steaks . . .' (she can get a bit carried away sometimes when it comes to food) '. . . the vast sleeping wonderfulness' (this bit was done with an arm gesture that barely missed a startled old lady) 'of the craggy mountains, snow-capped in the Northern Lights, looking down on the serenity as they've looked down since time began.'

I was about to point out there had been a lot of geographic shifts and things, and Scotland kept on having Highland Clearances and Jacobite Rebellions and Glencoe Massacres so the mountains hadn't been looking down on *anything* very serene since time began, but she got up and started pacing.

This is bad news because when she paces everybody ought to watch out. She's only little, but so are

7

guided missiles and she's got the same destructive effect when she really puts her mind to it.

'If our folks say we can't go,' I nodded warily, 'then we can't go. Let's be sensible. I know it's the holidays, but I haven't been able to get a job apart from walking that smelly poodle, which at 75p an hour isn't exactly going to turn me into a millionaire. *You* can't get a job apart from clipping people's hedges, and there aren't that many hedges around, and anyway you always get them squint. Old Frank's still wondering what happened to the ears of that silly privet bunny rabbit he was so proud of. So just *how* are we going to get it together? And what,' I smiled what I keep hoping will turn into my Mona Lisa smile (I have to practise a lot because of what that dentist did to my front tooth) 'would little Paulikins say if we *did* go?' (Paul is her current passionate partner.)

'Phooey!' She didn't exactly lift two fingers in the air but the overall effect was the same. 'Paul knows he can trust me. He knows he is the apple of my eye and *I* am the love of his life.' (Sometimes I think she's going to grow up to be an actress because she can even make eating an ice-cream dramatic when she wants to.)

'If I say we're going, then Jan,' she spun round and I huddled even further down the bench trying to escape the fall-out, 'we are *going*. All we need to do is earn the money.'

All!

Which is why I was standing on the corner of the High Street and Market Road at nine o'clock this morning trying to tell an American who was more confused than I where he could find things of beautiful and historic interest.

H has set us up in business, hasn't she? Complete with a manager who is a sidekick of Paul's and who, in my opinion, needs a side kick.

We are taking over where the Tourist Board and the council tourist service left off (not that I knew they had done). We are to be called *H & Co.*, have an office in her front room – because that's where the phone is – and advertise our services in the free paper, several shop windows and anywhere else we can think of.

Our services? Well, apparently we're going to give guided tours, tell people all about the town, point them in the right directions, enthuse about all our beautiful outlying countryside and the Giant Marsh Frogs – one of which I have never personally seen and I've lived here for nearly seventeen years – and generally do anything for anybody who's daft enough to pay us. Oh yes, and that includes posing at spots of hysterical interest for people with cameras who might want a twee memento of their momentous visit.

I can't see it, myself, but Tim – the guy who's been appointed as manager and co-ordinator of this little venture – gave me a telling-off for not being adventurous enough.

'No imagination,' he waggled his finger at me and I felt like biting it, then remembered my tooth. 'There's tons of scope for an operation like this. What we need to do is get you a kind of uniform so you're instantly recognizable and,' he started pacing and I groaned inwardly, two pacers are two too many, 'some badges. Then,' he got even more enthusiastic

9

and I got even gloomier, 'we need some advertising. I can easily organize that,' he announced grandly and H beamed at him proudly as if he were some kind of prophet instead of a prize twit. Paul, surprisingly, had the sense just to shrug. 'After that, all we have to do is wait for the phone to ring.'

'Jan, think about it!' He turned and looked at me and I suddenly noticed he had very brown eyes: not muddy-coloured like most people's, but really brown. 'Half the tourists who turn up don't know anything about things like The Carnival and The Silly Race and The Raft Race and The Festival. They don't even know where The Mermaid is, for Heaven's sake.

'How many times,' he came very close and I also noticed the way his mouth curved up at the sides as if it were continually wanting to laugh, 'in the last week have you been stopped and asked about The Mermaid?'

'On average, three or four a day,' I sighed, suspecting what was coming.

'And how many times have you been asked where the station is and how to get to the nearest car park?'

'Almost every time I go out.'

'Right again!' He looked triumphant and I decided despite the eyes and the mouth I didn't like him in the slightest. 'So start charging for that information and what do you get? Money, is what! And more than for your stupid poodle-walking!'

'There are just a couple of small points.' I decided I'd try to sound patient, though I didn't feel it. 'First off, it's probably illegal and we'll get done for soliciting or something.'

Everybody looked at me but I made myself steam on. 'Secondly, how's H's Japanese, Italian, Dutch,

Swedish, German, French and possibly Swahili, because I never knew she was bilingual. In fact she failed O-level French,' I can be nasty when I put my mind to it, 'and although I can manage the occasional *Oui* and *C'est là-bas*, I think Japanese might take me a bit longer.'

He stared at me thoughtfully then said, 'What did you do to your front tooth? It's wobbly.'

I blushed. I'm really very sensitive about that tooth.

'*I* didn't do anything. The dentist did. Now answer the questions.'

'Awh, come on Jan!' She was on her feet and pacing as well. 'If we tell the police what we're doing they'll turn a blind eye, and you've lived here long enough to know you mostly use sign language anyway.'

'Sure.' I was beginning to feel cross and I didn't like the way Tim kept looking at my mouth, but you can't talk with it shut unless you're a ventriloquist, so if he didn't like my tooth he'd just have to lump it. 'You can sign language somebody to The Mermaid. That's easy. But how do you tell some poor confused Italian what The Silly Race *is*? I mean, it's bad enough explaining it to somebody *English*!

'It won't,' I shook my head firmly, 'work. We're not experienced, for a start. *I* had to ask somebody the other day where the Methodist Church is and I felt a right twit because she turned out to be a visitor from Yorkshire and she knew while I'd forgotten!

'Anyway how're we going to pay for badges and uniforms when we can't even afford a Mars Bar? What happens if somebody wants to go to Smallhythe and see round Ellen Terry's place? *We* don't drive, do we?'

'No, but I do,' Tim interrupted me and I glowered at him. 'That's why I'm an essential part of the whole operation.'

'I think you need a licence to be a taxi!' I snapped and then ignored him – or tried to – and appealed to H. 'What do we do on rainy days when everybody dives back into their chalets in Pontins? And how's your mum going to feel about the phone being used all the time? As I remember it she had a fit over the last bill and threatened to put a padlock on it.'

'Nonsense. She was just having one of her funny five minutes. She'll be perfectly agreeable once she knows it's in a good cause.' H glared. I glared back. Paul tried to hide in his coffee mug. Tim frowned.

'*Please*?' Harriet Catherine Victoria Wyndham-Jones suddenly shot me her most appealing little-girl-in-trouble smile which can make strong men melt at the knees and old ladies pat her lovingly on the head. I tried ignoring it, too, but I knew I was on a loser. 'Please, can't we just *try*?'

'Oh, all right,' I sighed eventually. 'If you're that keen.'

She made up her mind and that was it. All I could do was straggle along behind.

Well, somebody had to pick up the pieces, and when she's in full flight, you never know how much is going to shatter where. Which it always does, because sometimes she can be a disaster area on legs, and I inwardly shuddered at what might be going to happen to a lot of our poor innocent tourists.

Chapter 2

So there am I and this poor confused gentleman in a
floral shirt, hung around with cameras, staring at
each other in a startled fashion. I am wearing jeans
and a white sweatshirt which is apparently going
eventually to have things printed all over it. H, I
know, is somewhere round Hilder's Cliff, also
wearing jeans and a white sweatshirt. Tim is lurking
because he wants to 'check progress and demand'.

'Ahem,' I cleared my throat and wondered if I was
panicking or getting hay fever, '*what* did you say you
wanted to look at, sir?'

'The Old Hospital,' the American drawled.

It was definitely panic and not hay fever because
my mind had gone completely blank and the only
hospital I could think of was the one at the top of
the hill.

'I think it belonged to a guy called Samuel Jeake
the Second.'

'Oh.' Total amnesia had definitely set in. 'Well,
that would be,' I waved vaguely, 'up there.'

'Mermaid Street, idiot!' Tim suddenly whispered
behind me. 'Hartshorn House.'

I managed to smile sweetly at the poor American.

'You need Mermaid Street, sir.'

I felt like hitting Tim.

'If you take your first turning on the left,' I waved
again and wondered how the Queen manages it all

the time, 'and go up Lion Street, then take another left turn, you should find it.'

He wandered off quite happily, then just as I was congratulating myself on my first customer – even if he hadn't actually paid me anything because he didn't know he was a customer – and beginning to breathe again, Tim grabbed me by the arm and shook me.

'Twit!' He looked fierce. 'If he does that he'll wind up by the Town Hall!'

'Listen,' I could feel my temper rising. It doesn't do that very often but since my very first encounter with Timothy Michael Dawson it was beginning to feel it was set on course to do it *very* often. 'I can't help it if I'm dyslexic. People can be with their rights and lefts you know. It's a well-accepted fact. And anyway, if you're so smart, why didn't you tell him yourself?'

'I was trying you out,' he said with a mysterious grin. 'That's what I'm here for, isn't it?'

'I don't know *what* you're here for! I don't know what *I'm* here for!' I almost wailed, much to the surprise of a passing pregnant prospective young mum. 'The whole thing's ridiculous. I don't want to go up a Cairngorm anyway and I can't ski! I'd be far happier sitting at home with a good book. Why don't you go and check on H? If you think *I'm* bad you wait till you find out what she's doing! She'll be sending people on day-trips round Dungeness, knowing her!'

'They're advertising those already,' he said in an over-patient voice. 'Just like Sellafield, so she can only help. Jan, why don't you just enter into the spirit of this thing. I'll be right behind you.' He patted me as if I were a puppy and I pulled away and glared at him. 'You don't have to get uptight and nervous about it. H has explained how sensitive you are, how you write poetry and go for long thinking-walks on your own.'

I glared at him again and made a mental note to wring H's neck.

'It'll work,' he went on. 'It's bound to work. Think about it. Two beautiful girls. Well,' he looked at my wobbly tooth doubtfully, 'more or less. Young. Willing. Smiling.' He gave the wobbly tooth another look and I wondered what kind of sentence you get for Grievous Bodily Harm. 'You'll become legends in your own lifetimes. An example to others to go out and do. The spirit of free enterprise and all that. The two *kids*,' he seemed to emphasize that last word a bit heavily and I glared at him again, 'who had the guts to do something for themselves over a summer so they could go somewhere in the winter without skiving off their parents. It's the stuff television programmes are made of. I can see it now,' he threw his arm in the air a bit like H and I had to stifle a giggle as he hit his hand on a brick wall, 'Television South – *The Two Brave Girls Who Made It.*'

Not for the first time I wondered if he was a complete nutter. He had this silly far-away smile on his face, which made him look reasonably attractive, I have to admit, but it was as if he was having a Close Encounter of Another Kind, and I don't trust people like that. H has it sometimes and it always gets *me* into trouble.

'Yes, well,' I shuffled uneasily, 'it's OK for you to waltz around like this, and it's OK for H to think she's going to make a fortune, but I have a feeling,' I suddenly realized he was holding my hand and I pulled away sharply, 'it'll all end in tears.' 'And they'll probably be mine,' I thought gloomily.

'Nonsense!' This time it was his arm that was round me and I squirmed away wondering where Paul had found him. I mean, Paul's barmy, but he's ordinary balmy and you can learn to cope with that kind of thing. Tim was definitely from another planet, which suddenly reminded me of something that'd been niggling at me.

'Never mind the nonsense.' I squared round to face him. 'You're not from round here, are you? In fact, you haven't even been here all that long, have you?'

'Nope.' He stuck his thumbs in the back of his jeans, which was a relief because I knew where his hands and arms were, and swayed forward on his trainers. 'London born and bred. The sound of Bow Bells, well Ealing actually.' He looked vaguely sheepish. 'The Big Smoke. But Mum and Dad decided to follow the Good Life – she writes, he paints,' he explained, apparently to the lamppost, 'and I thought I'd give it all a whirl. Got myself a job, too,' he stated proudly, while I opened and shut my mouth like a stranded goldfish, trying to get a word in edgeways, 'trainee in an estate agent's in Hastings. I could sell you a house, if you like.'

He looked at me and suddenly frowned. 'What's with the sudden interrogation?'

'Just how come,' I gulped, because he'd unhitched his thumbs and his arm had drifted back round by shoulders again which made me feel distinctly uneasy, 'if you've only been here a matter of minutes you knew where that house is? I've been here all my life and I *still* don't know where it is!'

'Ah!' He smiled again, tapped the side of his nose

with his free hand, and because of the way he looked I mentally reduced Grievous Bodily Harm to Attempted. 'I bought a guide book from The Martello, didn't I?'

It was so obvious I felt like kicking myself *before* I kicked him.

'Then why,' restraining myself from screaming was becoming extremely difficult, 'didn't you buy us one, too?'

'Wanted to test you out and anyway,' he shrugged, then looked sheepish, 'I didn't have enough cash. I don't start work till next month, and you don't exactly earn a fortune being relief behind a bar two nights a week.'

I could sympathize with that. I used to do washing-up in a pub that did meals at weekends until they decided the number of plates I managed to break was costing them a lot more than they were paying me, so something had to go and it made sense for it to be me.

'Well, I still don't think any of this'll work,' I grumbled, starting to walk towards the High Street. 'You don't know this town like I do. It's a soap opera on wheels with the locals and downright bananas with the tourists. They're either geriatric,' he had his hand on my neck and I shivered, I wasn't too sure why, 'or they're foreign language students, and either way you can't get much sense out of most of them.'

As if to prove my point a plump, bustling lady with one of those shopping trolleys drove it over his foot, and while he let go of me and hopped around in pain, I tried to stifle a giggle.

'Thank you, madam!' he shouted after her, and believe it or not she turned and beamed at him. 'So *sorry*, young man!' she shouted in one of those upper-class voices. 'Hope I didn't damage you?'

'Not in the least.' He smiled at her and I blinked. That smile was a little bit like the sudden sunlight you get down here after a storm — brilliant bright and with a sense of warmth you feel you can't quite trust in case it goes away again. 'My foot is yours to command.' He made a silly little bow and the plump lady blushed and laughed and gave him a half-wave before scurrying round the corner by Seeboard.

'Daft old thing! Nobody's probably talked to her like that in years.' The smile was still in position when it switched back to me. 'But maybe she won't run over so many people in future. Now come on.' His hand moved, caught hold of mine, and for some reason this time I didn't move away. 'Let's go and see how H is doing. You know,' he added conversationally, 'you two are the most extraordinary pair. *You* seem to follow like one of the marsh sheep wherever she leads. I think,' he strode up the hill determinedly while I panted after him and narrowly missed a collision with a British Telecom van, '*I* shall do some leading from now on. Then you can follow me for a change.'

I looked at him, and honestly didn't know whether to be excited — or to groan.

Chapter 3

There comes a time in the life of every young girl – or so I keep reading in all the agony columns – when she'd a) rather be anywhere other than where she is at the moment: b) wishes she didn't feel so confused: and c) just wants to stand up and scream.

For a couple of days after our momentous start when H managed to direct drivers *up* the Landgate – which was downright dangerous because it's a stretch of one-way street you can only go *down* – then forget where Winchelsea Beach is in what could only have been a moment of Paul-induced amnesia, *then* almost get us both drowned in the Tillingham trying to point out where the Raft Race started to a Chinese couple who definitely didn't speak English, I mostly wanted to scream.

My mum did when I stumbled in exhausted one lunchtime from running up and down Lion Street taking bunches of Lancastrians to St Mary's.

'What,' she said pointing a distinctly angry and trembling finger at the back garden, 'is *that*?'

I blinked sweat out of my eyes and peered through the kitchen window.

'It looks like a pony.'

'I *know* it looks like a pony! But what's it doing there eating my french beans?'

'I don't know.' I shook my head. I mean, as ponies go it seemed to be a perfectly nice pony, but they aren't exactly what you expect to find in a small cottage back garden. Then I had another look. I was feeling distinctly suspicious this time.

'Has – has,' I stammered because Mum was definitely not in one of her better moods, 'H been anywhere around.'

'She was here about five minutes ago and said she'd be back to see you. I popped out to get some milk and when I came back – that *thing* had its head in a rose bush!'

'Ahem,' an apologetic-sounding voice suddenly made us both turn round, 'it's all right, Mrs Braiden. It's only parked there temporarily.'

To give her credit, H did look uneasy. I mean, why she couldn't have parked it in her own back garden was one question, and what she was actually *doing* with it in the first place was the next obvious one.

'Then kindly *un*park it at once!' Mum exploded. 'In fact, you can unpark yourselves while you're at it,' she glared at me, 'before I commit some terrible crime and probably cut your heads off! Not that they seem to be very much use to either of you, any brains you might have been born with obviously departed for better accommodation long ago!' (She can be very sarcastic when she puts her mind to it, my mum. I don't think she's ever forgotten she once worked for a firm of solicitors before she married Dad and maybe something brushed off on her there.)

I sidled rapidly towards the kitchen door – I know when I'm not wanted – and H sidled right beside me.

The minute it closed behind us I heard Mum throwing things round the kitchen and winced. Supper would be another burnt-offering.

'Just what,' I looked at the pony – close up, it was

really quite big and it seemed to have an awful lot of teeth — 'is this doing here?'

'I'm looking after it for a couple of hours while its owner has lunch. I'm getting us ten quid for doing it, as well, only I was desperate to go to the loo and you can imagine how my Mum would've freaked if I'd put it in our place. I always thought yours was more reasonable,' she frowned and gave the animal a tentative pat. It just spat out a french bean at her and flicked its tail.

'Come on,' I said wearily, 'let's get it out of here. And for goodness' sake, H, don't do anything like that again or you won't have a best friend any more. You'll have a corpse.'

We plodded down to The Salts, because it seemed to be the only really sensible place to plod with a pony, and just as we were crossing Fishmarket Road H slyly said, 'Oh, I bumped into Tim about half an hour ago. He said he wanted to see you.'

'Oh.' For some reason which I didn't understand but which annoyed me I felt myself blush. 'Did he say why?'

'Something to do with maybe having a Boot Sale. But you can't have a Boot Sale when you haven't got a boot to sell from, can you?'

The pony nodded its head in agreement then started to chomp happily away at the rough grass.

'Maybe he's got a friend who's got a boot. Maybe he's buying a car. Maybe he's *bought* a car. If he's going to be a big, grown-up estate agent he's going to have to get around our dear downtown countryside, isn't he?'

Somehow I felt irritated. I'd had a cup of coffee with him in The Quayhole the previous afternoon

21

while H was trying to drown more tourists who wanted to look at the pretty boats and he hadn't mentioned a thing about cars, or much else, come to that. He'd just made me go through his version of Mastermind answering questions from the guide book.

'He really gets to you, doesn't he?' H leaned on the wooden railings and gave the pony another tentative pat. 'Well,' she twinkled mischievously, 'maybe it's the start of young *lerv*! And high time too, if you ask me. You haven't ever had a proper steady boyfriend, because you can't count that Robin-drip you kicked around with last year. At least Tim's funny and crazy and likes doing things. That other character just seemed to want to sit and hold your hand all the time.'

'Nothing wrong with that!' I snapped, though I admit, he had been a drip. 'And stop matchmaking, H. I don't think Tim and I are ever likely to be *lerv's*,' I imitated her, 'young dream. So just forget it. We spend most of our time arguing as it is. That's when he's not asking stupid questions about the date of the first church clock, which is about 1513, in case anybody asks *you*,' I said snidely, 'or giving me lectures about who was hung on Gibbet's Marsh. I am fed up' and I felt it, 'with all this further education. It's the holidays, for goodness' sake!' I almost wailed. 'And I don't want to go up a Cairngorm anyway!' The pony snorted agreement. 'I just want peace and quiet, and Tim Dawson isn't giving me it!'

'Somebody taking my name in vain?' a cheerful voice suddenly said. 'Talk of the devil, you know, and it's bound to appear!' A casual arm landed on my shoulders and started to steer me towards the children's playground. 'Now come along, young Jan. I want to have a chat with you, and H and her four-legged companion are due back at the cattle market at any minute.

'Don't run over any students, H,' he warned as he started to stride across the grass with me more or less in tow. 'Three coach-loads have just come in.'

'Oh goodie!' H caught hold of the pony's reins gleefully. 'French, Spanish or Italian?'

'French mostly.'

'Even better!' I groaned inwardly and wondered if emigrating would be a good idea.

'She'll be all right. Stop worrying about her.' Tim sat down on a swing and moved himself gently back and forward with his feet. He had very long legs, I noticed. In fact, taking him all-in-all he was long everywhere; apart from his nose which had a habit of wrinkling when he smiled, and his hair, which was nice and short apart from the bit that kept falling over his forehead. It was a funny colour for hair. I went and perched on the end of the seesaw hoping no little hooligan would come along and decide to shoot me up in the air by getting on the other end. I'm not keen on heights. He wasn't exactly mouse, he wasn't exactly brown, and he wasn't exactly blond, either – more of a mixture of all three.

'You,' he suddenly waggled a finger at me, 'are a terrible worrier, Jan. H is small enough and ugly enough to look after herself, so stop mother-henning her like you do. If she gets arrested we'll bail her out or send her a cake with a file in it or something.'

'If she gets arrested *you* can bail her out, or Paul can, rather. She nearly got me lynched this morning when Mum found that pony in the garden! I can't say I entirely blame her.' I chewed the end of my thumbnail thoughtfully. 'It can't be often you go out to buy milk and come back to find a pony chomping your scarlet runners.'

'Forget the pony!' Tim waved airily and a little kid who'd joined him on the next swing threw him a filthy look. I knew how it felt! 'Let's get to the matter in hand: the Boot Sale.'

'Do we have a boot?' The tide was turning and the weather was changing with it, which it frequently does. In about half an hour it was going to tip down rain, and I didn't want to be in the middle of The Salts in just a T-shirt and jeans; you can get awfully wet that way.

'Yes.' He got off the swing and came and joined me on the seesaw, which meant, of course, I went up in the air, so I glowered at him. 'I have bought,' he announced grandly, as if he were a Rothschild or someone, 'a car. I'll take you and show it to you in a minute. It's a bit of a banger, but it goes and it does have a boot!'

'Oh.' I felt a fool sitting in mid-air feeling seasick and I knew perfectly well, without looking, the kid on the swings was laughing at me. 'I thought you didn't have any money?'

'I don't. I borrowed it from Dad. He's just sold a couple of paintings so he's reasonably flush. I'll have to pay it back of course, which is another very good reason for getting our little organization working properly.'

'Tim,' I was in grave danger of losing my temper, or being sick, or both if I didn't get down from my dangling perch, 'I might concede to talk things over with you sensibly at ground level, but from up here it's a bit difficult.

'Right!' Next thing I knew my end had hit the ground with a resounding wallop and to say I felt evil as I sprawled to my feet is an understatement.

'OK,' I glared at him as he grinned at me, 'so we're going to have a Boot Sale. *Where* are we having this? When? And how do we afford to pay for the pitch? Oh, and how do we get the stuff to sell in the first place?'

'Come on.' He helped me get properly upright. 'Come and see the car. It's only just over the road.

'There's a sale going on on Sunday,' he explained as we tried to wend our way through the traffic coming from Camber down New Road. 'It's only a couple of quid or so for the pitch, and surely among the four of us our families have enough junk they can raise? Mine certainly has!'

Reluctantly I nodded. It wasn't such a stupid idea, really. One of my aunts did it out at Peasemarsh and raised forty pounds in an afternoon.

'All right.' I fell into step beside him. 'When Mum's calmed down I'll ask her what she wants to get rid of, and I'll have a look through my own stuff as well. But *please*, Tim,' I found myself facing him and very close, with my hand somehow clutching his arm, 'no more ponies in the garden! Promise?'

'Would you settle for a goat?' he asked too casually, and it only took me a split-second to realize he wasn't joking! 'Well,' he shuffled and went a bit pink under his tan, 'we've got to put it somewhere temporarily. I can't leave it tethered for ever in Eagle Road, and it'd only be for twenty-four hours. Very handy things, goats,' he tried to go on chattily, 'Cut the grass for you and suchlike.'

'Timothy Dawson!' I exploded. 'You are mad! Stark raving bonkers! Completely round the twist!' I tapped the side of my head. 'I don't even want to know *why* you've got a goat, let alone why it's in Eagle Road – the residents'll probably kill you, and they'd be right, that's a private road! I would very much like to live until I'm at least twenty, and if my folks find a goat in the runner beans or the rhubarb I wouldn't have a chance!'

'OK, OK, calm down,' he said placatingly. 'I'll ask Paul if it can go out on his Dad's field. I'm sorry if I've upset you. It was just a thought.'

'*Upset* me!' I stomped off in the direction of the Landgate. 'Oh, you haven't *upset* me, you've just started me off on a nervous breakdown! Ponies! Boot Sales! Now goats! When do the lions and tigers join in?'

I must've been flinging my arms about but I was so cross I didn't notice until a very soft stranger's voice said, 'I'm sorry. I didn't mean to get in the way, but this is quite a narrow pavement.'

I was quite prepared to jump down the voice's throat, too – until I looked up into the brownest, softest eyes I've ever seen.

'Is there anywhere round here I can get a coffee?' the voice, which I vaguely recognized to be Scottish, asked politely, and without being too clear what I was doing – or why – I nodded dumbly.

'Sure. I'll show you, if you like.'

I vaguely knew Tim was yelling at me about cars, that the wind had got up and that the inevitable rain was starting, but only vaguely, because the boy standing beside me was quite the most attractive thing I'd ever seen in my life, and now he'd walked into it I had absolutely no intention of letting him stroll out again.

Chapter 4

We managed to make it to the coffee shop just up from the police station before the rain came down in earnest, and I squiggled myself in to a vacant corner table feeling distinctly weak at the knees.

I'd already discovered his name was James, he was from somewhere near Perth in Scotland – wherever that is; I keep meaning to look it up on a map – that he was on holiday at one of the caravan sites in Camber, that he'd only arrived that morning, and that he kept getting lost.

While he was buying the coffees I watched him. Tall. Slim. Elegant, really, though I couldn't imagine him in a kilt. He was too sort of sophisticated for that (though I suppose all the Scots'll want to kill me for saying so). He already had the girl who was serving weak at the knees as well, and when he came back to our table and smiled at me I decided I really didn't have any knees left!

'So you're a local girl, then?' He sat down and pushed my cup and saucer across to me. 'What do you do?'

'Not a lot,' I mumbled. 'Well,' I had to be honest, 'H – that's my best friend – she and I are trying to make a bit of cash showing tourists the sights and generally helping them with problems. We're saving for a skiing holiday in the Cairngorms.' A Cairngorm suddenly seemed a very attractive idea indeed. 'Are they anywhere near you?'

'Not so very far,' he nodded. 'Not with the motorways and everything now. But I would have thought someone like you,' he smiled at me and my heart started doing very peculiar things in my chest, 'would have been wanting brighter lights and maybe even a foreign country.'

'Oh, well Scotland really *is* a foreign country, isn't it? To me, anyway,' I babbled. 'But the trip was all H's idea, so that's why we're trying to make some cash,' I ended lamely, knowing I couldn't really be making sense.

'And what about your boyfriend? Will he be going to?' James passed me the sugar and I stared at it as if I'd never seen brown crystals before.

'Boyfriend? *What* boyfriend?'

'That young man you were busy shouting at when I bumped into you.'

'*That* isn't my boyfriend!' I was having a very tiring day exploding all over the place. 'That's Tim! He's supposed to be masterminding our tourist operation, only he keeps asking me to do daft things like look after goats in the back garden! I don't,' I took a deep breath and tried to calm down, 'have a boyfriend as a matter of fact. I mean, well,' I realized I was about to start getting mixed-up again, 'I know a lot of boys who are *friends*, but I don't have one who's what I think you mean.'

'Oh.' He looked at me gently and took a sip of coffee. 'Well there's another surprise now, isn't it? Someone like you, and no boyfriend. Ah well, the world can certainly be a funny place.'

'Listen,' I suddenly felt suspicious, 'are you sending

me up or chatting me up, or what? You've got awfully personal awfully quickly.'

His face crashed — that's the only way to describe it. He sat there with a cup half-way to his lips looking like a wounded puppy.

'I'm terribly sorry if that's what you're thinking,' he stuttered. 'I wouldn't dream of such a thing. In fact I never normally talk to girls at all, at least,' he added hastily, 'not strange ones. But there's something about you, something that's different. But please excuse me if I've offended you in any way.' He glanced quickly towards the big glass windows of the café and then began to push his chair back. 'The rain's stopped. I'd best be on my way before I say anything else wrong. Thank you for your company and for showing me this place. Perhaps I'll see you in the town sometime while I'm here.'

Almost without realizing I'd done it I reached out and grabbed his arm.

'No, please.' I smiled and hoped he wouldn't notice my wobbly tooth which was wobbling even more than usual. 'You don't have to go. It's all my fault. I've just had an exasperating day and I'm a bit touchy. Sit down and finish your coffee, then maybe I can show you round the place a bit — if you'd like me to, that is?' I added doubtfully.

'I'd like that very much indeed.' His smile came back and I gave an inward sigh of relief. 'It isn't much fun having a holiday on your own. The guy I was supposed to be coming with broke his leg in a football match and as we'd paid the deposit and everything months ago it seemed a shame to pass the caravan up. It's just that I don't know where to go or what to do, for I'm not much for amusement arcades or lying on the beach all day.'

'Well,' I took a deep breath and marvelled at whatever was making me behave like this, 'you could always tag along with H and me if you like. I don't mean all the time,' I added hastily, 'but you'd get to know the town and meet people. Quite a lot of Scots come here as a matter of fact.' I seemed to be raving but I couldn't help it. 'Tim gets in the way quite a bit. That's the guy I was shouting at,' I explained over-patiently, 'so if you could get him off my back I'd be grateful! Paul, H's fella, works during the day, but we all meet up at H's in the evening usually. There isn't really a lot you *can* do in Rye after five o'clock, there isn't a cinema or anything, except during The Festival when they show arty films at The Community Centre.' This was turning into a much longer speech than I'd intended so I gulped and rushed on. 'I'm sure you're welcome to join us if you want to.' I crossed my fingers on the last bit because a premonition of impending trouble quicksilvered through me, but I mentally shooed it away and decided to ignore it.

'You're very kind.' He reached across the table and took my hand, which did funny things to my insides. 'Very kind indeed. And of course, if I can be of any help . . .'

'Well,' I tried to make myself sound light-hearted, but the trouble still seemed to be firmly impending, 'there's always a goat in Eagle Road you could babysit, though whether it would fit in your caravan or not, I don't know.'

'A goat.' He looked thoughtful. 'Useful things, goats. My granny used to have one in her back garden; mind you, it was a big back garden, more of a field, really. She used it for eating the thistles. It was called Hamish, as I remember. But why've you got this goat anyway?'

'I don't know,' I muttered in extreme resignation. 'These things just happen to me when H and Tim are around. It was bad enough when it was only H, but Tim's barmier than she is, and that's saying something!'

'Come on.' I got to my feet. 'Let's go and see if we can find them, then I can introduce you.'

'All right.' He got to his feet and eased himself round the corner of the table. 'But if you're really stuck with this goat I could always put it on the field behind the caravan, provided we could get it there. I'm sure nobody'd mind.'

A sudden vision of sitting in an as yet unseen old banger of Tim's nursing a goat and jolting towards Camber made me giggle and I shook my head.

'Not to worry, James. I was only joking. Anyway, the thing's probably had a parking ticket by now and been towed away to wherever you tow illegally parked goats. I sincerely hope it has. And I, for one,' I joined him on the pavement, 'am not going to bail it out!' Then we started to walk down the street together in the companionable way you do when you feel as if you've known someone all your life.

Chapter 5

We finally caught up with H in Church Square and she didn't just raise one eyebrow when I introduced James and tried to explain how I'd found him. She raised both of them, then gave me an extremely odd look indeed. That was when I realized James was holding my hand and smiling at me proudly.

'*Tim*', H emphasized the name unnecessarily, 'is looking for you. He said, if I bumped into you, not to worry about the goat, he's had it moved. But he also said to tell you he's calling an extraordinary general meeting at my place tonight to decide on the Boot Sale. You will', she smiled sweetly, a darn sight too sweetly which is a sure sign of the impending trouble I'd suspected, 'be able to make it, won't you? I mean, young Lochinvar here isn't going to spirit you off and wine and dine you somewhere exotic, is he?' She had the audacity to smile sweetly at him, too.

'Don't be an idiot, H!' I snapped, feeling embarrassed for poor James (and at the same time managing to get my hand out of his). 'And of course I'll be there. What time?'

'Half-six. Paul'll be back by then. Will Rob Roy', another gooey smile which made me want to strangle her, 'be joining us?'

But James just smiled back and shook his head. 'Not tonight.' For a second I thought he was going to get his own back and say 'Josephine'. 'I have to get myself some provisions and sort out the caravan.

'Jan,' he turned to me and gave a funny little nod, 'you've been very kind. If I were to be in the town tomorrow where might I find you?'

'Oh, around.' I gestured vaguely, then felt guilty. After all, I'd been the one who'd suggested he join H and me in the first place. 'Tell you what,' inspiration struck, 'I usually go home for lunch.' I dived into my purse, found a tatty bit of paper and the stub of pencil I've started keeping so I can write down directions for people who don't understand what I'm saying. 'If you're around, try there.' I scribbled furiously. 'Say about half-past twelve. But if Mum answers the door looking as if she's going to bite someone, pretend you're a travelling salesman who's got the wrong address. Anything! It'll only mean she's found a baby elephant in the back garden this time!' I shot a sarcastic glance at H who shrugged and apparently became totally fascinated by a window-box full of drooping petunias. Then I handed the paper to James who smiled, gave a funny little bob of his head and said, 'I might just do that. I'll see how it goes. Now I'd better get myself down to the supermarket I noticed in the High Street before they close. Do they stock porridge, would you think? And maybe baps?'

'Yes.' H deserted the petunias before I could answer, and this time she wasn't just gooey, she was dripping charm like it was going out of style which I most certainly didn't trust. 'And if you want to go the whole hog, the butcher further up the High Street catches his haggis live daily and also sells mutton pies.'

'Whatever next!' I was no longer sure who was

sending up whom. 'I never knew the haggis ran all the way down here. You learn something every day! I'll be seeing you.' Then with a cheerful wave he turned on his heel and strode off through the church yard.

'Just *what*', H and I said together as we watched him disappear, 'is going *on*?'

'Nothing's going on as far as I'm concerned,' I added, glowering at her.

'Have you gone off your head at last?' she glowered back at me, totally ignoring my last sentence.

'What're you talking about, H?' I suddenly felt very tired and rather damp from getting wet earlier.

'You turn up with some Scottish drip who's clutching your hand like you're his mum on his first outing to Woolworth's, you stand around with a silly-looking smile on your face, then you give him your address when you've known him less than twenty minutes! You could get murdered in your bed, or worse! You leave poor Tim stranded in the middle of The Salts, call him all sorts of things, and then invite Scots Wha' Hae, or whatever he's called, to come and join us!'

'I thought', I tried to sound sarcastic, 'you were all in favour of the Scots. "All those Scottish guys in kilts",' I quoted back at her, ' "all that vast sleeping wonderfulness . . ." Perched on a Cairngorm in your après-ski in the middle of a ceilidh. That's what got us into this stupid lark with tourists and ponies and goats! What's suddenly changed?'

I realized we were very probably at the start of our most serious row ever.

'You're a twit Jane-Anne Braiden! *That's* what's changed! You can't see further than the end of your nose, and considering how short your nose is, that isn't very far! I know,' she was stomping, not pacing this time, 'you are extremely inexperienced with the opposite sex, which is hardly my fault because I've done my best to introduce you to them. I know you would rather sit at home and cry your eyes out over some soppy novel. I know, though you'll never admit it, you actually *like* Atlantic Star and Whitney Houston, and even Johnny Mathis, for goodness' sake! And if I ever hear 'You Don't Bring Me Flowers Anymore' I'll probably throw up! *Wise* up, Jan. It's 1988 and a local hero your James ain't! He's more a throw-back to the Middle Ages. In fact, he probably spends his time in a cave half-way down a cliff watching a flipping spider, like whoever-it-was!'

In all the years I've known her I've never seen her so angry – not even when John Davis floated a plastic spider in her Coke one lunchtime, and that was bad enough (H hates spiders).

'Listen,' I took another deep breath – I seemed to be doing a lot of that that day – 'just what has got up your nose so much? James is just a bloke I happened to bump into. He wanted a coffee, so I took him to The Patisserie because he doesn't know his way around. . . .'

'*You* don't know your way around!' She glared at me. 'He's a wallie. And *you're* going to get involved over your neck! If we had any available heather you'd find yourself lying in the foggy-foggy-dew, or whatever it is, with your knickers round your neck and a prescription for the Pill in your other hand. Well I', she stopped stomping and faced me, 'don't happen to want that to happen to a friend of mine. Streetwise you are not. A disaster area you are turning into.'

'*I'm* a disaster area?' I gulped like a goldfish running out of air. 'How about you? You've got Paul. The pair of you are positively embarrassing sometimes when you decide you've got to have a cuddle. I don't *want*', I tried to calm down, 'all those fellas you keep trying to throw at me, and you're not exactly tactful about it. You're my best friend, but you're not my entire life, and you're not entitled to *run* my life, so if this disaster area here,' I pointed at myself, 'happens to find somebody for herself, which I haven't,' I added quickly, 'then what are you so uptight about? Shouldn't you be happy and jumping around for joy that I may no longer be your responsibility?'

A very elderly man with a stick, whom I vaguely recognized, threw us a very peculiar look, and I could almost hear him saying inside his head, 'Younger generation!' in a more than tutting voice.

'All right.' H shrugged. 'Suit yourself, but I thought you had *some* sense. Tim, if you'd take the time to see it, has fallen for you hook, line and whatever the other bit is, and believe me he's worth more than that touch of tartan you were holding hands with! Just don't say I didn't warn you. That's what friends are for.' She glared at me fiercely. 'See you at half-six, with or without the tartan wonder, because believe me, you'll have him following you around like a tame poodle, and you *know* what I think of poodles!' Then she strode off – she didn't pace or jump up and down, she just strode, and 5′ 7″ of H striding is something I've never seen before – through St Mary's churchyard, leaving me feeling like a distinctly confused wet weekend as the rain started to pour down again.

Chapter 6

I didn't go home immediately. I went and sat on a bench by the side of the church instead and tried to ignore the fact that I was getting soaking wet and would very probably catch pneumonia.

'Well if I do,' I grumbled to myself, 'it'll be all H's fault. I mean, how can she judge somebody like that after thirty seconds? And where did she dredge up all this nonsense about Tim from?'

I felt miserable and lost and a bit like bursting into tears. A little black cat with a curious expression on its face crept out from under an acacia bush and stared at me suspiciously, then scurried over and wound itself through my legs miaowing, as if it were as upset as I felt.

'What d'you do?' I asked it, and it gave another miaow. 'There's nothing wrong with James that I can see. He's only here on holiday and he's lonely. Anybody staying by themselves in a caravan out at Camber would be lonely!'

'But,' a little warning voice inside my head whispered suspiciously, 'he did latch on to you pretty fast, didn't he? And wouldn't most people if they'd seen you were in the middle of a row with someone else just've walked on by? And why was he all smiles for H when he met her, *and* the girl in the coffee shop? Is he just a bit *too* charming?'

'Oh, what the heck!' I stood up abruptly and the

cat scurried back under the acacia, for which I didn't blame it in the slightest. 'Whose life is it anyway? If I'm making a mistake then I'm making a mistake, but I'd be making an even bigger one if I listened to all H's twaddle about Tim.'

I was still mentally muttering to myself when I pushed open the back gate, and I wasn't a wet weekend anymore – a drowned rat was closer.

'Jane-Anne Braiden!' Mum looked up from the cooker which she'd obviously been wrestling with. 'Are you entirely without any common sense? Go and get changed and have a shower at once. I've got enough to do without having you snuffling round the place with a summer cold. Oh, and,' I was just about to trail upstairs, miserably wondering why everybody had decided to start calling me by my proper name, when she shouted after me, 'that young Tim rang. He said to tell you he'd be round to collect you at six. Perhaps I'll get a chance to watch EastEnders in peace. Your father's working late. Damn' the thing!' I heard her swear, so I stopped trailing and did a fast sprint to my room. Mum and the new halogen cooker never really have got on, and if she was still fuming over parked ponies they'd be getting on even less: she isn't exactly what you'd call a naturally enthusiastic cook.

I peeled off my wet things, dumped them in a heap on the floor, then shivered my way into a dressing gown.

I didn't want to see Tim. I didn't want to go to any extraordinary meeting. I didn't want more benefit of H's advice on my non-existent relationships with the opposite sex. I just wanted to curl up in a corner and expire quietly.

I padded gloomily across the landing to the bath-room, towelled my hair and made faces at my disgusting self in the mirror. I was too thin. Once, when H had been cross with me over something, she'd accused me of being anorexic until I'd pointed out she was the one who kept dieting while I was the one who kept eating, when Mum's eccentric cooking allowed, that is. My hair needed cutting. In fact my hair needed a *style* instead of being a hopeless bird's nest. I had a flat chest and stumpy fingernails. No wonder the opposite sex and I didn't exactly connect! I was a catastrophe on legs looking for a disaster area and I didn't like myself in the slightest.

'*Jan!*' Mum yelled up the stairs just when I'd started the shower going. 'There's someone with a funny voice called James on the phone for you, and he's in a pay-box so you'd better hurry up.'

I groaned. I couldn't help it. Right at that moment I didn't want any Jameses complicating issues, either.

'I don't know what you think you're up to, young lady!' A floury finger waggled at me warningly as I plodded into the hall. 'Who's this now?'

'Just somebody I met this afternoon. He's on holiday at Camber Sands.' I reached out for the receiver wearily. 'And he isn't foreign. He's from Scotland.'

'Scotland! That's all I seem to hear about these days,' Mum tutted, then beat a hasty retreat to the kitchen to the sound and smell of something boiling over or burning – or both.

'Hello, James,' I muttered, and the local line did its normal crackle which partially deafened me, 'what d'you want?' (All right, it was ungracious, but I didn't feel gracious, and also I was freezing to death, mainly due to our household's belief that even if it's snowing it's still summer and the central heating has to be switched off.)

'Jan,' he drawled softly, and my heartbeat went up again, 'I was wondering if maybe I could hire your professional services for tomorrow? I'll pay,' he chuckled. 'Don't believe a word about the Scots and meanness. It's just that I was thinking of having a bit of a tour round and you'd be the best person to show me where to go.'

I bit back the obvious reply to that and said (I hoped) calmly, 'Tour round what and *in* what?'

'Oh,' he sounded genuinely surprised, 'I've a motor-car. Did I not tell you? It's my father's, but it goes,' he added incongruously. 'Would you be interested in the idea? I was just thinking of looking at some of the countryside.'

'Well, I'm afraid the daily rate is twenty pounds,' I babbled, pulling the figure out of thin air (we didn't have a daily rate), 'and that would have to include snacks if it were *all* day, I'm afraid,' I added, wondering why I was saying all this.

'Twenty pounds seems very reasonable,' came the reassuring voice. 'And I'd pick you up of course.'

'*Jane-Anne Braiden!*' Mother suddenly thundered through and grabbed the telephone from me. 'Whatever you think you're doing, you're not! Daily rate, indeed!' She'd either overheard me or been listening on the extension and got everything wrong. 'My daughter,' she exploded into the telephone, 'is a decent, well-brought-up girl, so whoever you are young man I suggest you leave her alone before I call the police.'

'Mum!' I almost laughed. She looked so silly and

frustrated and tousled. 'He just wants a guide to the countryside for the day, not what you're thinking at all!'

'Well,' she handed the phone back to me reluctantly, '*I* want to see him first. How do I know he isn't a dirty old man, or a rapist, or a pervert? Or worse!' I didn't know how much worse you could get than all that, but I nodded at her reassuringly and she flounced away again.

'I'm sorry about my mother,' I apologized. 'She's cooking and she gets a bit fraught when she's doing that. Would ten o'clock at the house be all right? You'd better meet her, otherwise she'll put a bulletin out on Police Five or something!'

'Ten o'clock'll be just fine. I'll look forward to it. I'll bring a picnic if I can catch one of those haggis your friend was talking about. See you in the morning, then.' I could see his smile and my legs suddenly went peculiar again. 'Take care now.'

The line went dead with its normal squawk and crackle and I sat down heavily on the bottom step of the stairs. I just didn't know if I liked the prospect of spending an entire day with James or not, but at least it would get me away from Tim and H – and somehow that suddenly seemed like a very good idea.

Chapter 7

Drawing a very thick veil, or preferably a black-out curtain, over the extraordinary meeting would also be a good idea because everybody argued with everybody else.

H paced and called me a twit, an idiot, a wimp, a complete wallie, and one or two other things which shouldn't be repeated.

Tim strode and kept looking at me sternly.

The over-all vote – i.e. H and Tim – went in favour of the Boot Sale, and it was only when H started for the hundreth time on what a non-starter James was going to turn into that Paul woke up and said anything at all.

'If Jan wants to go out with somebody then it's her business,' he yawned. 'You've got no right to interfere. She's old enough not to need a nursemaid, so stop behaving like one.'

H stopped pacing and glared at him.

'Jan doesn't know which end is up!'

I began wondering if I might be invisible, considering I was sitting directly in line with her route across the carpet.

'Jan', Paul said quietly but firmly, 'has a life of her own and you shouldn't organize it for her. Goodness knows, you try to organize everybody else's – *and* you make a mess of it most of the time – so why don't you just pack it in?'

I gawped at him. He'd never talked to H like that before and they'd been going around together for months.

'If this James-bloke is a disaster, then he's a disaster,' Paul went on, 'but he's Jan's disaster, not yours, so stop interfering. I know', he stretched and rubbed his eyes, 'precisely what is churning round in that little mind of yours and much as I love you, I think, you'd be a lot better advised to keep out of things.' H's jaw dropped in total disbelief. Tim sat down with a perplexed frown on his face, and I was by then quite sure that, not only was I invisible, I quite probably didn't exist at all.

'You can't', he went on obliviously, though he was definitely in the H danger-zone, 'just organize someone's life forever because it suits you that way. You can't make Jan fall in love with Tim or Tim', he glanced at him and Tim abruptly turned away, 'fall for Jan. They're *people*, H, not pieces in some mental jigsaw of yours.'

One of those long drifting silences wandered over the room and nobody looked at anybody else. I wanted to scream at H, tell her I wanted my best friend back and that this whole load of nonsense was a hurricane in a thimble. Tim looked as if he wanted to strangle something, probably me, and H stood there with clenched fists.

'All right,' she said suddenly in a strung-up voice, 'I will never organize anything or anyone again. But don't say I didn't warn you.' She nodded in my direction. 'I've got first-hand experience on things like this, remember?'

'H,' I wasn't entirely sure what she was on about but suspected it had something to do with her dad, although she never talked about him, 'I'm not even going *out* with James, for Heaven's sake! I accidentally bumped into the guy this afternoon, we had a coffee together, he wants a guide for tomorrow – and suddenly there's a three-act drama going on! Why?' But even as I asked that a small, very small but extremely irritating, thought charged across what was left of my brain and I knew if I didn't voice it I'd regret it. '*I've* never been jealous of you and Paul – or you and anybody else come to that, even though I never did like Michael. So why're you acting like you're jealous now?'

'I am *not* jealous.' Ice cut through the pin-drop quietness. 'I just don't want you to make a fool of yourself and get hurt. I've seen what happens when people get hurt and it isn't very nice.' Then without another word she turned on her heel and walked out.

Tim appeared to be making a mental thesis on the joins in the wallpaper, but Paul opened his eyes and shook his head like a bemused Old English Sheepdog. I just sat, wondering if I was going round the twist and trying to stop a cold, dead feeling sneaking into my stomach.

None of us spoke for a long time then Tim very quietly, and surprisingly, said, 'Hitting nails on the head like that maybe isn't such a good idea, Jan.'

'What d'you mean?' I gulped and wondered if I was going to cry.

'H *is* jealous, it's patently obvious. In a peculiar way I haven't worked out yet, so am I. But if you've found somebody for yourself then, like Paul says, it's your business and you should be allowed to get on with it whatever happens in the end. H is just', he shrugged unhappily and incongruously I started to like him again, 'feeling excluded. She's more or less had your undivided attention for a long time now. Right, Paul?'

Paul nodded benevolently. 'Trouble is,' he suddenly smiled at me, 'we all know how extrovert and unpredictable H is, but nobody really knows Jan because,' (I was getting very close to throwing something) 'you've been tagging along in H's shadow for so long, and now you've decided to do something for yourself, by yourself, everybody's confused — H most of all.'

'I just wish everybody would understand', I fumed as quietly as I could, 'that *I am not doing anything!*'

Unexpectedly Tim came over and patted me on the shoulder as if I was a stray dog (which nearly made me bite him). 'Be yourself,' he said quietly. 'That's important. And if Paul's right, which I think he might be, find yourself. H'll recover.'

I got to my feet, I'm not sure how, and sort of staggered towards the back door. All I wanted was to be out of range of anyone's well-intentioned advice, and all I needed was to be on my own.

Chapter 8

And that's thankfully precisely what happened.

Mum had obviously given up her unequal battle with modern technology because I found a note propped up against a suspicious-looking casserole of something I didn't even want to recognize saying she'd gone round to her sister's because she was fed up (I knew how she felt) and would I please not let the woodstove go out.

Now the fact the woodstove had even been lit meant it actually was as cold as I'd thought it was earlier, because the woodstove controls the central heating and also the entire household because it has a tendency to be temperamental if not fed vast amounts of logs and Coalite.

I groaned and looked in the log basket hopefully. No logs. So I shivered my way out to the back garden, loaded up a pile and dragged them indoors wondering where Dad got his sudden inspiration to have the blasted things installed from.

I felt a bit like Cinderella, poking at the glowing embers, and I suddenly and very positively did want to cry. I kept seeing Tim's face in the flames, then James's, then H's. They all leapt and danced around at me, so I shut the stove door quickly and wandered through to the kitchen. I didn't trust the casserole, in fact I wasn't even hungry, so I wandered out again and wondered if killing myself might be a sensible idea.

I couldn't get in touch with James to stop the day's sightseeing. I couldn't ring up H and have a moan at her because she wouldn't be talking to me. I didn't know where Tim and Paul were likely to have got to, and I didn't exactly fancy going down to The Community Centre and hanging around there in case I bumped into anyone I knew. In the end I sat down and tried to read one of Mum's magazines, but I had to go and start on a harmless-looking short story about a dog who lost its owners because they both got killed in a car crash, and that just finished me. By the time Dad came in I was in floods of tears, my face felt as puffy as a balloon and the woodstove was quietly expiring because I'd forgotten to put any logs on it.

'What on earth', he switched on the main lights, 'is the matter with you? Where's your mother? Why's the stove on – or nearly on, I should say – and who's the young man who thrust this at me on my way up from the station?'

He handed me an envelope while I sniffed and snivelled.

'And *what*', he came back out of the kitchen pointing behind himself at the casserole, 'is *that*?'

'I – I don't know,' I hiccuped. 'And Mum's round at Anne's. And I'm crying because,' I stopped and tried to focus on the envelope, I didn't even recognize the writing, 'well, just because,' I ended lamely, realizing I wasn't even too sure myself.

'Oh.' Dad put his briefcase down and shouldered his way out of his jacket. 'That makes everything perfectly clear, of course. Now could you also take the trouble to explain why the kitchen looks like the aftermath of Hiroshima,' – I hadn't even noticed – 'and why the two women in my family are behaving in a somewhat erratic fashion?'

'Mum got mad at me because H temporarily parked a pony in the back garden, and you know what she's like with the cooker when she gets mad,' I sighed wearily.

'Hence', sometimes the fact that my father works with computers can make him sound very pompous, 'the reason for what would appear to be sausages swimming in tomato-coloured gravy?'

'Yes.' I nodded.

'And why', he asked over-patiently, 'a pony in the back garden?'

'I don't know.' I shook my head this time.

'And why', he sat down beside me and took my hand, 'all the tears? Mum's cooking leaves a thing or two to be desired, I'll admit that, but it isn't *so* bad, Jan. Sometimes she gets it right.'

'It's not Mum!' I started dripping again. 'It's H. We've had a row. She isn't speaking to me and I don't think anyone else is either and I've got to give somebody called James a guided tour tomorrow and that's what seems to be wrong and I'm going to bed!' It all came out in a rush and I stumbled to my feet. 'I'm sorry,' I heard myself say. 'But I wouldn't touch that casserole if I were you.'

'I don't intend to. I'll boil an egg, if we've got an egg. Then I'll go and collect your mother and try to find out precisely what's been going on. The adolescent in question', he'd obviously had a bad day, too; he always uses words like that when his programmes haven't programmed properly, 'said his name was Tim. I've never seen him before in my life, but he appeared to be tethered to a goat and certainly knew who I was.'

'Oh no!' I didn't believe anything any more. 'Not the goat again! Just don't mention goats or ponies to Mum when you find her, Dad, or neither you nor I'll grow to be old and grey!' Then I turned and still clutching Tim's envelope, fled upstairs.

The letter, note, whatever it was, was scrawled on a grubby piece of paper that looked as if it had been torn out of some kid's exercise book, and I suddenly realized I didn't even know if Tim had any brothers or sisters, or where he lived, or what his father painted or his mother wrote or which estate agent he was going to be gainfully employed by. To be honest, I realized about the same time, there was an awful *lot* about everything I didn't know.

Dear Jan, it read, which was straightforward enough; it was the next bit that threw me into a panic. *This is just to say I'm sorry if we all spoke out of turn and hurt you in any way but it's because we're all very fond of you. After you left H came back practically in tears. I think she'd like to see you soon. But if you ever feel you need another friend you can contact me at this number. Don't lose it because it's ex-directory and the exchange won't put you through. I was talking to my mother about you and she said she'd like to meet you sometime, she writes for teenage girls' magazines among other things* — presumably as an agony aunt, I thought glumly, and Tim reckoned I was the agony — *so let me know. Have a good day with your James tomorrow* — MY James! One cup of coffee and he was MY James! Was everybody raving or was it just me? — *and we'll hope to see you soon. Love, Tim. PS I am taking the goat back so don't worry.*

I read it. Then I re-read it. Then I wondered if standing on my head and squinting at it sideways would make any more sense of it. Then I gave up and just sat there holding it feeling increasingly bewildered. For all Tim was dotty and kept having hare-brained ideas, he was also intelligent and that letter read like something H might've written in one of her worse moments. She doesn't, as they say, have much of a way with words. In fact she drives our English teacher bananas and the only postcard I've ever had from her just said, 'Love, H' followed by three Xs.

Another of those niggling little doubts that kept niggling wriggled through me and I looked at the writing again. It definitely wasn't H's, it was too neat but, the niggle turned into a positive itch, how had Tim known who Dad was or where and when to find him? Why was everybody hoping to see me soon, as if I were going to vanish off the face of the earth? I mean, Rye isn't exactly huge. Everybody bumps into everybody else sooner or later, except on Tuesday afternoons when it closes down. What had Tim's mum got to do with anything, and didn't he realize that if the word got around about something like that we could practically consider ourselves engaged? And why bring the goat into it? I'd denied all responsibility for the goat, hadn't I? The itch grew into a positive suspicion and I was just about to go downstairs and use the phone when I heard Mum and Dad, busy arguing, come in.

'I will not have ponies, parked or otherwise, David!' Mum was saying fiercely. 'Or bunny rabbits, or stray kittens, or any other livestock! This is a house, not an animal sanctuary! H is getting worse, not better, as she grows up, and I don't want Jan thinking she can join her! What with this Tim boy, and now this James boy, I really don't know if I'm coming or going!' There was a crash, which probably meant the cooker was suffering again and I winced. Then Dad said reassuringly, 'All I mentioned was the girl's obviously very upset and it might be a nice idea if you went and had a chat with her. Maybe she's having a difficult time of the month or something.'

That did it! I abandoned telephone calls, got changed as fast as I could into my long T-shirt, turned off the light and hid my head under the pillow. One of Mum's, 'When you're older and have more experience, dear . . .' numbers was something I couldn't face.

She did look in eventually, but I gave a little muttering moan, as if I were asleep, and she went away again muttering, presumably to assassinate the casserole, or Dad, or both.

Although I didn't expect to, I slept, but I had a peculiar dream about being chased by a human-sized limpet which could talk and wanted to know the way to Appeldore, though why it wanted to get there it didn't seem to know.

Unfortunately, when I woke up next morning, it was brilliant sunshine and I groaned. I'd been half-hoping for torrential rain or a hurricane or anything which would've put a stop to James's picnic and given me a chance to find H. But dead on ten o'clock while Mum was writing out her shopping list and trying to pretend she wasn't watching me pacing, the doorbell rang.

'That'll be your Scottish friend, I expect,' she

murmured while I headed for the door and wondered how I'd got myself into any of this.

He was standing there with a smile that does things to my knees – and promptly did again – holding a bunch of red carnations.

'H-hello, James,' I managed to stutter. 'Come on in.'

'These are for your mum.' He held out the flowers. 'I thought she might like them.'

If anybody knew how to butter parsnips he did, and I knew precisely how Mum was going to react.

I was right.

She took the flowers and promptly melted at him.

'What a kind thought,' she fluttered while I tried not to giggle. Sometimes Mum looks and acts younger than H and me (usually when she's had a couple of G & Ts on a Saturday night), but James just smiled a bit more, she melted a bit more and I wondered if her knees had gone peculiar, too.

'Would you like a cup of coffee, ahem, James? Oh and please, do sit down.'

'That would be most pleasant, if it's no trouble, Mrs Braiden.' He was pretty quick on the uptake because I knew I hadn't told him my last name so he could only've caught it while Mum was squawking over the telephone the previous evening. 'And what a nice place you have. It's almost French with all the wood, so warm and mellow.'

Nobody's ever called the cottage almost French before – quite a lot of other things but never that one.

'Oh, thank you!' Mum was now glowing instead of melting. 'It's small, but there are only three of us. Which part of Scotland are you from, James?' She sat down, still clutching the flowers, while I dangled around like a lost length of string. 'Do go and put the coffee on, dear,' she said without looking at me, so I wandered through to the kitchen and clunked the kettle noisily.

When I came back with the tray they were nattering away as if they'd known each other for years and Mum was explaining how she'd once actually been to Perth – which was the first I'd heard of it – and how magnificent the Tay and the bridges and the North and South Inches were. It all sounded double-Dutch to me. I mean, how can you have a north and south *inch*?

'Aye, it's a bonnie place, but it's terribly changed, Mrs Braiden. Terribly changed.' He shook his head dolefully, 'And in the summer it gets so full of the tourists you can hardly move.'

'I know how you feel,' I heard myself say sourly and wondered if I was about to have a mood. 'You wait until all the coach parks are full here and you want to get down the High Street in a hurry. If you don't get jostled to death you get elbowed, and if you get away without suddenly disappearing under a car, you can thank every lucky star you've got!'

'I suppose so.' He looked downright mournful. 'But I've been thinking for a while now a change is as good as a rest. To tell you the truth, Mrs Braiden,' he turned and smiled at Mum again, 'it's one of the reasons for me deciding to come here still. I've heard about everything they've been doing with the airport at Lydd, y'see, and it sounds – well,' he shrugged charmingly while Mum beamed and hugged her flowers, 'as if there would be great possibilities, so I thought I would like to look into the matter at first hand.'

For some reason I couldn't quite put my finger on my heart did a quick nose-dive. James at Lydd and Mum with that soppy look on her face tended to lead me to believe all could well stop being right with my world – or at least mine and H's – and I wasn't at all sure I wanted that.

'Come on, James.' I clanked a coffee cup noisily. 'You're burning up the day. If you want to have a look-round we'd better go.

'See you later, Mum.' I picked up my bag and a sweater and headed for the door. 'Oh, and if H rings tell her I'll phone her back, please.'

Mum threw me one of those motherly looks which mean 'have a good time dears' then stood up and held out her hand to James, who took it – and for a moment I wondered if he was going to kiss it. 'Have a good day.' There it was! 'I hope we see you again, James, and thank you for the flowers.' Then she leaned over and kissed me on the cheek. I hate it when she does Queen Mum impersonations like that, it makes me feel all iffy. 'Be kind to our guest, dear.' (I also mistrust it when she calls me 'dear' because it usually means I'm doing something right for once). Then with another little royal wave she sailed through to the kitchen to look for a vase.

'Well, well,' James said once we were out on the pavement, 'what an attractive and young-looking mother you have, Jan. Now I can see who you take after.'

'Oh.' I wasn't too sure *how* to take that one, or even if I wanted to take it at all.

'You're a very attractive young lady.' I realized

he'd got hold of my hand again and one of our elderly neighbours was giving us a peculiar look.'In fact you look particularly fetching in that outfit. Now, where are you going to take me? The car's just down here, by the way, and I've the picnic in the back. I told the traffic wardens I wouldn't be long and they said it should be all right.'

For a second I wondered if he meant the picnic or the parking, but then he was holding open the passenger-seat door of a metallic Renault Gold for me with a little bow. I nearly curtsied back, but I'm not sure how you do that in jeans so I just tried to clamber in as gracefully as I could. Trouble was, my legs suddenly seemed to have sprouted and I got in a tangle with my handbag and then the seat belt, but it finally all connected with me in a bit of a heap and James beside me, beaming.

'Right. Where to, Madam?'

'I'm only the guide,' I heard myself bleat pathetically, wishing Tim were around, 'but if we take the Camber road I can show you Dungeness. It isn't open today for visitors, only Thursdays. Then we can go through Lydd, as you're interested, and then if we head for New Romney and turn off towards the sea, just after there it's quite pretty at Littlestone and Greatstone. The sands there are good and we could have lunch. Then,' I took a deep breath and blessed Tim for all his questions-on-the-area sessions, 'we can either go up to Dymchurch and on to Hythe, or head across the marsh, down to Appeldore, on to Brookland and pick up the main road home.' I felt like an ordnance survey map. 'How would that suit you?'

'You're the boss.' That hand came over and patted

me on the knee. 'Here we go. A life on the open road!'

We didn't actually say a lot. I kept mumbling about where things and places were supposed to be and crossing my fingers I'd got it right. James kept nodding his head and smiling and occasionally holding my hand – and Tim's silly face kept swimming around my brain until I wanted to scream at it to go away.

When we got to Littlestone and parked I walked James up to the funny tower-thing nobody quite seems to know about, then he rubbed his hands together and said, 'Lunch! I know it's early, but you go and find us a nice spot and I'll go and get the things. It's too beautiful a day to be driving *all* the time.'

I clambered over the wall and plonked down in the nearest available spot. There weren't all that many people around, considering the time of year, so I amused myself watching a young couple who reminded me of H and Paul playing with a puppy.

I wanted, I thought gloomily, to be part of a couple, too – with or without the puppy, but I wanted it on *my* terms. I wanted, I closed my eyes because it really was hot, despite the sea breeze, to be swept off my feet with champagne and caviar (even though I'd never tasted the stuff), bought red roses and adored from the same feet up.

I half-opened one eye and glanced at my feet. As feet went they were perfectly practical for getting around, but I couldn't exactly visualize anyone wanting to drink champagne out of my trainers.

'Wake up, dozy!' The lilting Scottish voice with its smile was back. 'Lunch. Oh, and a small thing for yourself for doing me the honour you're doing.'

I didn't just wake up. I sat up – straight up.

James was standing there with a thick travelling rug over one arm, a hamper that was like one of those things only people who shop in Harrods have, and he appeared to be struggling with two red roses wrapped in cellophane and finished with a twiddly bow.

I closed my eyes again, convinced I was back in bed with the giant limpet about to get me any moment.

'Here.' He knelt beside me and gave me the flowers. 'Red roses for a very nice person who took the trouble to befriend a stranger. I couldn't afford a dozen, and anyway they only seem to sell them in tens these days, must be something to do with inflation or the balance of payments.

He was busy spreading out the travelling rug and unpacking the hamper while I sat there like a right twit clutching these flowers and wondering what to do with them – well, how many times've you been given red roses on a beach just off Romney Marsh on a hot summer's day? 'I couldn't afford champagne, either, but a nicely chilled Hock should go down quite well with cold chicken,' the chicken appeared on a plate, and not a paper one, either, 'salad,' it came out in a china bowl complete with wooden salad servers, 'cheese. I didn't know if you liked Stilton or not, but this one smells sufficiently like old socks to be quite good. Anyway,' he smiled again while I was still blinking, 'if you don't, there's a nice piece of farmhouse cheddar. Choccies for afters,' he held up a box of Bittermints, 'but we'll keep them out of the sun. Oh yes, of course. Fresh strawberries.' Another china bowl.

'James! Where on earth . . . what on earth . . . how

on earth . . . ?' I spluttered, feeling increasingly out of my depth.

'I brought most of this down with me because I didn't know what to expect in the way of shops and things. I got the strawberries and the cheese this morning. Why?' he looked suddenly crestfallen. 'Would it be all wrong for you? Are you maybe vegetarian or something?' He handed me a paper napkin, spread out cutlery and salt and pepper and started to uncork the wine.

'No, I'm just', I leaned back again, 'overwhelmed! I've never had a picnic like this in my life!'

'Then there's a first time for everything, and I'm afraid I'm not one for sand in the sandwiches and potato crisps out of packets.'

H was never – I blindly took the plate he'd carefully arranged for me, and it was real, too – going to believe this. H was going to say I had gone off my trolley, had hallucinations and ought to see a doctor.

'Tell me about yourself, Jan.' To my continuing surprise he suddenly leapt to his feet, unzipped his jeans, shrugged out of them and then pulled his T-shirt over his head. Then a very nicely-muscled brown body, not that I'm an authority on these things, in trunks sank down on its front on the travelling-rug and started to chew a chicken leg.

'There's nothing much to tell,' I muttered, and ate a piece of chicken breast. 'I was born and brought up here. I'll probably die here.' I waved vaguely in the direction of Rye. 'I'm doing A-levels, but I don't know what I want to be before you ask. I like children and animals, though not necessarily in that order,' I added hastily, just in case he was having any strange ideas. 'Mum wants me to be a teacher. Dad says I should suit myself. I can't', it was the first time I'd ever positively thought of it, 'ever really see me leaving this area, not to live anyway. There's something about it all', I stared along to the White Cliffs, 'that gets you. The mists, the marshes, even the damn sheep! You can walk up to the top of Hilder's Cliff in the town,' I hastily explained because I realized he probably wouldn't know what I was talking about, 'early on an Autumn evening just as the sun's going down, and if it's a clear night you'll see straight across there.' I pointed at the Channel in front of us. 'If there's the mistiness you can watch it creep to begin with and then sort of billow.

'Most of the time when the tides change on the Tillingham and the gulls come in or go out there's a weather change. The winds can be awful. The snow can be even worse, we keep getting cut off in the winter, everybody thinks they know everybody else's business, but I, well, I love it,' I ended lamely.

'Very poetic.' James carefully tucked his chicken bones into a clean polythene bag and wiped his hands.

'Yes.' I nibbled a tomato glumly. 'H calls me that, too.'

'Ah, but she's a different kettle of fish, isn't she?' He sat up and put his arm round my shoulders. 'Wild. Cheeky. Mischievous. Maybe even a wee bit unhappy.' It wasn't a question, it was a flat statement and I glanced at him sharply.

'Maybe.' I had to nod in agreement. 'But then we all are sometimes, aren't we? And she's got Paul.'

'While you've got no one? Is that it?' The arm was pulling me closer and when he kissed me I didn't know whether to panic, struggle, scream, kick him — or just let myself be kissed.

In the end I let myself be kissed. He tasted of chicken and salad and white wine, with a lingering hint of toothpaste.

'I'm sorry!' He suddenly pulled away. 'I shouldn't've done that. I do apologize. Have a strawberry.' He held out the bowl. 'Or a Bittermint. It's just that I', he looked as confused as I felt, 'get lonely, too. I've never been any good with girls. They all seem to think I'm after one thing. They all seem to think', he sounded bitter and when I looked at him his profile had a funny little smile twisting round the lips, 'you can't just be *friends*.' He sighed and I wondered what to do or say next. There was something just not quite right somehow and H would've got herself out of this in no time. But then, H would never've got herself into it in the first place!

'James,' I said gently, 'talk about yourself. I mean, why d'you want to come down here from Scotland? Why Sussex? Why not London or,' I scrabbled round in my brain for another big town, 'Birmingham or Manchester?'

'Och, I wanted a change, that is,' he frowned at me, 'I *want* a change. I've been training to be an actor.' The smile suddenly switched back on like a spotlight and several warning bells went off inside my head. 'But I don't think I'm much good at it.' The warning bells rose to alarm level, and I could've sworn I heard H laughing '*I told you so!*'

'That's why I thought,' he took my hand, he seemed to be getting very attached to that hand, 'something else, something different, a new place, new environment, new people,' the hand was firmly squeezed and I nervously ate two strawberries in quick succession, 'because you can't live without people, can you? They're what life's all about.' You can't argue with that so I just sat there and kept quiet. 'I want to settle down, get married, have kids'. The smile again and by that time I was wondering how long it would take me to swim to France, because by that time I'd had the terrible sneaking suspicion that H's first summing-up had been right — and probably that James was a far better actor than his teachers, or whoever, realized.

'Ahem, I think we'd better make a move,' I said, managing to extract my hand and shove it behind me out of the way. For some reason I felt clammy and uncomfortable, as if I'd been selected for something without being consulted first.

'Whatever you say,' he smiled, but this time it didn't have quite the same effect. Then he got to his feet and gazed across the sea like *The Boyhood of Raleigh* (or whoever it was), and intoned dramatically, ' "*They that go down to the sea in ships, that do business in great waters, These see the works of the Lord, and his wonders in the deep.*" '

He looked quite beautiful but I gave a quick shudder and decided the best — and probably safest — thing was to get home just as quickly as possible. Unfortunately I made the mistake of reading out of the guide book that Ellen Terry's house was at Smallhythe and the car nearly skidded into the ditch in excitement, so we spent hours plodding round this National Trust place while he oohed and ahed over costumes and daggers and books.

'James,' I touched his arm and he promptly took my hand, 'I really should be getting back now if you don't mind. Tea and things, you know,' I gestured vaguely. I didn't feel in the least bit like tea, but it was the only excuse I could think of.

'I'm sorry.' He immediately looked contrite. 'How selfish of me. And after all you've done, too. We'll go at once.' He suddenly stooped and kissed me on the cheek, which made me go pink and a couple of Americans go 'Awh, how sweet.'

'Will it be all right if I see you tomorrow? he asked as we walked back down the grass verge to the car. 'Maybe we could go somewhere else? Another picnic. Or I could take you to lunch,' he added hastily.

Good old-fashioned panic grabbed hold of me. 'I – I'm not sure what's happening tomorrow,' I stuttered. 'I have to see H and Tim first. They may've organized something.'

'Of course, of course,' he nodded sympathetically. 'Then I'll ring you, if that'll be all right?' There wasn't a lot I could do to stop him as I'd given him the number, so I nodded back dumbly. 'And thank you again for everything.' This time the kiss was more of a nibble in the region of my ear and I began to seriously wonder if I was allergic to boys because I didn't like it in the slightest. In fact, for all he was wonderful to look at I had a suspicion I didn't like James in the slighest. He was just a bit *too* perfect. A bit too good to be true with none of – for no good reason the name flashed through my head – *Tim's* rough edges. He should've been every girl's dream. Instead it felt as if he were turning into this one's nightmare.

Chapter 9

Now just about everybody in Rye, apart from the tourists or the couples who've decided they need a charming olde worlde weekend retreat, is related to everybody else. There are one or two exceptions but they're pretty few and far between. So imagine my not-a-lot-of-surprise after James had dropped me off when I bumped into Paul's aunty Dorothy, who's vaguely related to Dad.

'I hear you've got a new boyfriend, dear!' she gushed, waving her basket full of bits and pieces around and disturbing a perfectly happy snoozing cat. 'How nice!'

'I never had an *old* boyfriend,' I practically barked and the cat twitched its ears. 'And I certainly don't have a new one! He's just another tourist who wants to be shown around.'

'Ah,' she said knowingly and smiled. 'Well he sounds a very nice young man, bringing your mother flowers like that.'

'He's a *very* nice young man,' I tried to sound sarcastic. 'Now Dot,' changing the subject as quickly as possible was the only way out of this one, 'd'you happen to know where Paul, Tim and H might be lurking, because I want to unlurk them.'

'Well,' she considered, 'Paul and Tim are playing snooker tonight, dear.' Half a cabbage nearly hit the cat, who wisely decided discretion was the better part of valour and took off for quieter places. 'I haven't seen H at all.

'Jan,' she peered short-sightedly at me, 'are you quite all right? You seem to be a mixture of flushed and pale which makes you look rather peculiar.'

'I'm fine.' I wasn't. I was tired, full of Ellen Terry, sand and chicken, about to develop a foul temper and an even fouler headache, and although it was only five in the afternoon, I felt like going to bed and turning into the Sleeping Beauty (only I didn't want to be kissed by any handsome frogs and Mum would probably only've woken me up with bowls of nourishing broths every two hours, which didn't seem fair on the cooker).

I said goodbye to Dot, wandered round to H's and rang the doorbell. When her mum finally answered she stared at me as if I'd just arrived from outer space and was closely connected to E.T.

'She's gone for a walk. She said she wanted to think,' Mrs Wyndham-Jones said. 'I don't know what's the matter with the pair of you. You look dreadful and I've never heard of H wanting to think before!' Neither had I but I let it pass. 'She muttered something', Mrs Jones went on, 'about going across the marsh to Winchelsea and catching a bus back. Is that any help?' I groaned inwardly, nodded, thanked her very much and wandered off again.

I knew precisely where H would be. It was where she always went when something upset her, and by the time I actually caught up with her she was leaning on a farm gate apparently having an intense conversation with two sheep.

'You look terrible,' she said comfortingly when she noticed me.

'I *feel* terrible!' I snapped. 'But if anybody tells me how I look I'll strangle them. Why did you have to go off and think today? Why couldn't you just be at home with your feet up in front of the telly, the way you normally are? And what're you thinking about anyway?'

'Things,' she said mysteriously.

'What things?' I sank down on the grass and dangled my feet in the reeds, but some insect bit me on the ankle so I undangled them again.

'All sorts of things.' She squatted beside me and started shredding grass. 'How was Robert Burns? Did he attack your maidenly virtue?'

'He did nothing of the sort!' The grass was damp, which after yesterday's rain was hardly surprising, but I couldn't be bothered to move. 'And he's called James, which you perfectly well know. And right at the moment if I never see him again it'll be too soon! And we had chicken and Stilton for lunch, and strawberries and Bittermints,' I wailed, 'and I feel sick!'

'I'm not surprised,' she said calmly. 'Was it all on one plate or were there several?'

'Oh shut up, H! None of it's funny. James seems to think I'm the only girl in the world he can rabbit on at, and believe me he can rabbit! There's nothing actually *wrong* with him, he's just a. . . . a. . . .'

'Wimp?' she supplied.

'I think so,' I nodded.

'Well I shouldn't say I told you so, but I told you so. Now d'you want to go and jump in the ditch yourself, or will I give you a helping hand? Mind you,' she peered over the reeds, 'there's not a lot of water in it but a marauding toad might attack you if you're lucky.'

For no real reason, except that she was being H, I giggled and looked at her. That was when I realized she'd been crying.

'Of course you might get stung by a dragon-fly or devoured by a passing duck,' she added thoughtfully, 'but I'm sure we can manage a nice obituary in the free paper. Would you like red roses or white ones?'

'H,' I touched her on the wrist, 'what's up? What's happened? It's not you and Paul, is it?

'What on earth're you talking about?' she said too brightly and started plaiting grasses together. 'You know, we could make an absolute fortune if we could learn how to make corn dollies. We could sell them all over the place.'

'H,' I tried sounding patient, 'never mind the corn dollies; anyway you make them out of corn, not grass; just *what* is the matter?'

'Oh,' she threw the grass into the ditch, 'you! Paul! Mum! Everything!'

'OK.' I took a deep breath. 'Me I can understand. Paul I don't think I want to know about. But what on earth's wrong with your mum? She seemed perfectly normal when I saw her. She hasn't had another phone bill or anything, has she?'

'No.' A solitary tear dripped down the side of her nose. 'She's got a boyfriend — well, a man friend — well, this bloke.'

'What's the matter with that?' I scrabbled in my pocket for a tissue and handed it to her. She took it and sniffed. 'I'd've thought you'd've been pleased. She's not exactly ancient or anything, is she? And she must get lonely sometimes.'

'The matter is,' another tear plopped, 'I can't stand him! And, well – but you mustn't tell anybody, Jan – I've been writing to Dad. He was going to come down next week. I was, well, sort of hoping they'd get together again. Now I just don't know *what* to do because Mum seems really stuck on this bloke!'

'Oh.' There wasn't a lot else I could say, so I said it again. 'Oh.'

Then we just sat there staring gloomily at the horse-flies while I wondered if anything anywhere could get into any more of a muddle.

'How,' I hesitated, 'how long've you been writing to your dad, H?'

'Since he left. He asked me to. He said I was the only real thing he had and he didn't want to lose me. I love him, I think. Not the way I love Paul or anything like that. It's deeper down inside. I can't explain it. It's, well,' she looked even smaller than normal, 'more permanent, I suppose. But I love Mum, too. I care about her the same way I care about you, I guess.' The plopping had turned into a good imitation of Niagra Falls. 'I don't want either of you to be hurt.'

'H, you are one great idiot!' I gave her a quick embarrassed hug. 'You can't go around protecting people from themselves, or whatever else it is you think you're doing, for the rest of your life. You're not one of those funny humanitarian charities. We've all got to make mistakes. Even you.' Niagra Falls had turned into torrential rain.

'Come on.' I struggled up and pulled her to her feet. 'I'm sick of being bitten by funny things. I'm also tired. I never want to see another cold roast chicken in my life, and if I don't get home and wash the sand out of my hair I'll go completely round the bend.

'I don't want to know about you and Paul,' I warned as we started back down the footpath. 'That's between you two to sort out, but I think maybe *we'd*', I glanced at her and she snivelled - I've never seen her snivel before, thinking obviously wasn't good for her — 'better try to sort out the other mess. *Tomorrow*,' I added sternly. 'With no parked ponies, galloping goats, boys, men or anything else. OK?'

It was the first time I'd ever put my foot down so firmly and to my amazement she just blinked at me and nodded. 'OK,' she whispered. 'And Jan,' she suddenly got fascinated by her feet which appeared to be scuffing themselves together as if they wanted to kill each other, 'I'm sorry for everything I said.'

'What about everything you wrote?' It was a long shot but I had to try it.

'Oh, that!' Her feet got even more agitated. 'You mean you guessed?'

'H,' how can you really be exasperated with something like a dripping rain forest — 'I *have* known you since we were quite small, remember? Shakespeare you are not, and I may be a dope but I'm the one who passed the English Language exams. Why on earth did you con Tim into writing it?'

'We-ell,' there was a puppyish sort of yelp, 'girls aren't supposed to say all that to other girls if they're normal, are they? And we're both normal, and I didn't know what else to do,' she trailed off.

'Anybody can say anything to anybody as long as they mean it, so for goodness' sake stop going on. We're *friends*, remember? Mates. Buddies.' I kicked a stone and a rabbit suddenly shot out of a bush. For some reason it reminded me of James. 'That's what's important. One day,' I sighed, 'I suppose we'll both get married to somebody. One day we'll both be sitting somewhere with squawling kids talking about the price of disposable nappies and how to cope with chicken-pox. But we'll still be friends. Now please stop acting like a wet weekend.'

She nodded obediently into her fringe, then kicked the same stone I'd been kicking.

'Tim said to tell you,' she muttered a bit too casually, 'he and Paul'd be finished about ten tonight and if you wanted to see him all you had to do was knock. I don't know what he means. Do you?'

I had a sneaking suspicion, but just for once I wasn't going to say anything, because I wasn't at all sure what I was going to do about it.

Chapter 10

What I did do in the end was mumble some barmy excuse at Mum and Dad about needing fresh air and wandered off out into the darkness. Actually it wasn't really dark, there was still a bit of a glow in the sky over towards Dungeness, and the wind whipping across The Salts did freshen me up.

I sat in the Gun Garden, huddled into myself, and tried to make sense of everything, but the trouble was none of it added up, however hard I tried to make it.

Somehow or other, just because I'd got mad at Tim and flounced off, I'd got landed with James who was just too – well, nice.

Somehow or other H's dad was coming back which seemed to be upsetting a lot of applecarts, although I didn't understand why. He could only be coming back because he wanted to come back, couldn't he?

Somehow or other H and Paul had had an upset, but they were having upsets all the time so that wasn't really anything new. Tomorrow or the day after they'd be back together as if nothing had happened, and knowing H the chances were nothing serious had happened anyway.

Somehow, I bit my lip and wondered if this was what the posh papers call 'the trials of adolescence', I couldn't work out how I felt about Tim. One minute he made me so cross I wanted to scream, then the next – when I thought about him – I felt a faint flickering glow, a bit like watching a candle in the wind.

'There aren't any problems, there are only solutions,' I muttered to myself grumpily, then remembered Mum going on about what a pleasant boy James was and touching her carnations gently, while Dad threw me doubtful looks and was obviously deciding to run me through his computer to make sure I was all right.

I was fussed – there wasn't any other word for it. Everything was rushing towards me at once like leaves in a gale and I didn't know which bit to try to cope with first.

'I thought you might be here,' a familiar voice behind me suddenly said. 'And I'm not going to ask if you had a good day because if you'd had a good day you *wouldn't* be here, you'd be dancing a Highland fling or something. H rang and said she'd seen you. She seems to be in a state about something.' Tim sat down beside me and stared out towards the Channel as well. 'Want to go on sitting, or go for a walk, or come home and have a coffee, or just be by yourself? I can always disappear again.'

'Let's just sit.' I didn't even look at him. I didn't have to, and suddenly that was important. 'I'm glad you came.'

'Oh, good.' A hand touched mine briefly, then was gone again. 'You're not into eating people tonight then?'

I shook my head and something suspiciously like a sigh escaped from my chest. 'I don't normally eat people anyway. I don't normally lose my temper and rant and rave. And I *never* go around picking up strange boys.'

'Well, there's a first time for everything,' Tim said calmly. 'Life's full of surprises, or so they tell me. The most surprising thing in mine is that the car got through its MOT today. We can go out in it sometime, if you like? And I promise I won't bring a picnic with cold chicken.'

Suddenly I laughed. 'H told you about that, did she?'

'She mentioned something to the effect she didn't think you ever wanted to see a chicken alive or dead again.'

'And d'you know,' for some reason everything was easy and relaxed, I could feel the tension drifting away from my shoulder blades, 'what Mum had for supper? Salad and . . .'

'Cold roast chicken!' we chorused together.

'Sod's law!' I felt Tim shrug. 'Did you eat it?'

'No. I discreetly filed it in the bin while everybody was watching the news. And I'm afraid I didn't have one pang about the starving millions in Africa either, though I should've done I suppose,' I said as an afterthought.

'I don't suppose your little bit of chicken would've stopped world famine,' Tim murmured thoughtfully. 'I mean even Bob Geldof must throw things away sometimes. What happens when he forgets he's defrosted the fridge and then finds a bit of liquid lettuce lying in the salad crisper?'

'D'you think he does defrost his own fridge?' I asked hazily. It was a peculiar conversation, but somehow it seemed absolutely natural.

'If he's got a fridge, somebody's got to defrost it,'

Tim answered logically. 'Though Mum leaves ours until it's like one of those glacier mints polar bears sit on.

'Talking of Mum,' he turned towards me, 'when're you going to come and meet her?'

'Sometime,' I said vaguely, 'What does she want to meet *me* for anyway? There's nothing very special about me, and I'm not,' I felt myself begin to blush, 'your girlfriend or anything.'

'Never said you were,' he mumbled. 'Mum just likes meeting people, that's all. She likes to keep in touch with her readers, because she keeps saying she's the oldest teenager in the business.'

A fantastic vision of Mum in a leather mini and stilettos rocketed across my brain and I tried to blink it away.

'Oh, don't worry.' He reached out and squeezed my hand quickly, as if he'd just read my mind. 'She's perfectly harmless, apart from when she's working – then she mutters a lot at nothing in particular.

'I have to admit,' there was a little laugh in his voice and I wondered if he was sending me up, 'she does call her typewriter George, and she has some kind of love-hate relationship with it Dad and I don't understand. She loathes cooking, and she can't see without her specs – though she won't admit it – but apart from that she's fairly harmless.'

'Oh.' She sounded like a variation on my own mother, and I caught myself wondering if I'd be the same when I had a home and family of my own.

'Anyway, think about it.' Tim stretched lazily. 'Oh, but if she offers you any apricot wine say you're a teetotaller. It's disgusting!'

'Oh,' I echoed back at him, realizing his arm had

gone along the back of the seat and his hand had drifted naturally on to my shoulder. It felt familiar and comforting, as if it should always be there, and for no good reason a cloud of panic pounded through me.

'I think I'd better get back, Tim, before the red alert goes out and Dad launches Operation Jan. He gets very protective sometimes,' I gabbled.

'OK,' Tim said easily, and the arm withdrew, which left me feeling lost. 'Would you like to go out tomorrow? Paul's got the day off. The four of us could go and be tourists somewhere.'

I shot a suspicious look, but I think it was too dark for him to see.

'Where did you have in mind?'

'We could go swimming off the famous Camber Sands,' he said mischievously. 'I could hold your hand and pretend to be deeply in love with you, and then if any bonnie Scots were around they might think about somebody else to feed strawberries and chicken to!'

Despite myself, I giggled. 'You're evil!' I got to my feet. 'Let's take a rain check on it in the morning. I'll ring you.'

'OK,' he said again, then found my hand and held it firmly. 'Don't lock yourself away, Jan. Butterfly about a bit. H may be mad as a hatter, but I think she gets more out of life than you do.'

I thought about that as I trudged through St Mary's churchyard, which didn't look at all the same since the big maple tree disappeared in last year's hurricane. I hadn't really been aware I did lock myself away, until he'd said it. When H was busy or just wasn't around I spent a lot of time in my room playing tapes or reading, or just downright daydreaming and I knew that sometimes worried Mum because she'd have the occasional tut about me not getting out enough. But it didn't worry me. I quite liked my own company, and I could always talk to myself inside my head – in fact I've had some very interesting conversations with myself. But locking myself away? That was different. That sounded serious, and I'd have to think about it.

Unfortunately, when I let myself in through the kitchen any thoughts I had careered out the window – because James was sitting there in the armchair, with a glass of beer at his elbow and a settled sort of smile on his face.

Mum was simpering, which is always a bad sign, and Dad had his eyes shut behind *Computer Weekly*, which basically meant he'd given up. The television was blaring out gloom and doom from somewhere.

'Oh there you are, dear.' Mum looked up brightly when she heard me close the door. 'James popped in on his way back from Hastings. Isn't that nice?'

It wasn't nice at all as far as I was concerned, but I dredged up a smile, pinned it on my face and nodded. 'Hello, James.' Sparkling conversation. 'How was Hastings?'

'Very quiet, I thought, but then I don't know how Hastings usually is. I was going to go to a movie, but there wasn't really anything I fancied, so I thought, well, Rye's on the way back,' I couldn't really deny that, 'take a chance and see if wee Jan's at home.'

I winced and even Dad opened an eye in surprise.

'James was telling us how he's training to be an actor.' Dad closed his eye and went back to sleep again. 'It sounds fascinating, but such a *precarious* career.'

'Ninety-five per cent of the profession out of work at any one time, Mrs Braiden,' James sighed soulfully, 'That's why I'm thinking of turning it all in and doing something useful with my life. The social services, maybe. Or working with the disabled. Acting's all very well if you want to be showing off all the time, but it doesn't really help people.'

Mum glowed agreement. I felt sick. And *Computer Weekly* gave an ominous rustle.

'Well,' he drained the last of his beer and got gracefully to his feet, 'I'd better be getting back to my little grey home in the West!' It was obviously a joke so Mum and I smiled accordingly. 'Will I be seeing you tomorrow, Jan?' I caught the full blast of his smile which, I was beginning to realize, he could turn on and off like a tap, and before I could weaken under it I shook my head violently.

'Uhm, afraid not. I have a date.' Mum's eyebrows shot through her perm and *Computer Weekly* gave another rustle. 'That is,' I garbled on, 'I have to see H, and Paul and Tim. We've had an arrangement to go off for the day for ages.' I crossed my fingers behind by back and hoped I didn't look as guilty as I felt. I'm a very bad liar. 'And Tim wants to give his car a test run.' Mum's eyebrows climbed even higher and I tried to ignore her. 'Also,' I took a deep breath, 'I have to meet Mrs Dawson, Tim's mum,' I threw in by way of explanation, 'because she writes about people like me and she likes to keep up to date on what she's writing about,' I limped off lamely.

Everybody, including Dad, was looking at me as if I'd gone right round the bend, and I stood there shuffling from foot to foot. It's surprising how large your feet can grow when you're in the middle of what feels like a crisis of conscience.

'Och well,' James gave me an understanding pat on the shoulder, 'not to worry. I'll give you a ring and maybe you'll be free later in the week.

'Mrs Braiden,' he gave that funny little half-bow, 'I thank you for your hospitality.

'Mr Braiden,' he held out his hand to Dad who took it and shook it, looking bemused, 'it's been my privilege to meet you, sir.

'Jan,' the smile flooded and he grabbed my hand as if it were a lifeline, 'I cannot thank you enough for the pleasure you gave me today.' Then with Mum parading along beside him as if she'd been hypnotized he headed for the front door.

'Just *who*', Dad exploded as they stood and yattered at each other in the corridor, 'is *that*? Where on earth did you find him? And would it be at all possible for you to lose him again?'

'I hope so.' I sat down, feeling drained. 'I bumped into him, literally, yesterday, and I took him on a sightseeing tour today. For money. For this skiing holiday. But Dad,' I heard myself wail, 'he's like a – a leech! He seems to think I'm the only person in the world for him!'

'And are you?' Dad got up and poured himself a whisky, which he very rarely does.

'I don't think I could ever be.' I felt about five years old and as if I'd just fallen over and cut both my knees. 'He's fabulous to look at, and he's kind and he's generous, but,' I shrugged, 'it all feels false, somehow.'

'Your mother likes him.' Dad knocked back his

drink and poured another one, then he crossed towards me, put his arm round me and gave me a bear hug. 'Don't worry, sweetheart. These things happen. As your Nan would say, it'll all be the same in a hundred years' time. But I must admit,' I could feel him smiling down at me as I snuggled against him, 'if you've got to get involved with anybody – and sooner or later I suppose you will – I'd prefer that scruffy individual who met me at the station to Young Lochinvar or whoever he is. He is completely boring. Now get yourself to bed. You look all-in. Oh, and Jan,' he sat down in his chair and rustled his newspaper embarrassedly, 'what *did* you do with the chicken salad, by the way?'

I giggled suddenly. I couldn't help it.

'Guess.'

'Very right and proper, too,' he nodded understandingly. 'I've never liked chicken salad anyhow, and there was a slug in the lettuce.'

Then just as I was heading towards the stairs he looked up from his glass and blew me a kiss. 'Be yourself, Jan,' he murmured. 'Because whether you believe it or not you *are* in there somewhere, and I think you're quite a nice person. Don't get messed around.'

I looked at him, feeling closer to him than I ever had in my entire life.

'Thanks, Dad,' I whispered, then as we heard Mum give one final coo and the front door close I raced for the comparative security of my own room.

Chapter 11

The next day was brownish-grey and miserable. So was I. I woke up sneezing and carried right on sneezing through that awful muesli stuff Mum insists I have for breakfast.

'You've got a cold,' Mum said helpfully, in between fighting with the washing machine.

'I do I've got a code,' I snuffled miserably. 'By dow half of Rye probably dose I've got a code!'

'Take some paracetamol and go back to bed then. Summer colds can be dreadful and the last thing I need is you dragging around under my feet all day.'

I glowered at her and uncharitably hoped the washing machine would bite her, but I had to admit going back to bed and hiding under the duvet seemed an excellent idea, so I sneezed into the last of the muesli and watched with interest as flaky bits of it spiralled into the marmalade.

The wind gave what Nan calls 'a keening wail' round the chimneys, and a couple of jackdaws – like black torn pieces of paper – sailed past the window on their way to nowhere special, which was where I honestly felt I was going. I sniffed and wondered what had happened to the summers. When you're little, five or six or so, they always seemed to be full of sunshine – but maybe that was just an illusion. Maybe all you remembered was the sunshine.

I shambled to my feet and plodded upstairs to the loo.

Looking at myself in the mirror as I was cleaning my teeth was even more disgusting than the way I was feeling.

'Jan Braiden,' I sneezed again, 'you're a mess!' Then for no particularly good reason I sat down on the edge of the bath and howled my eyes out . . .

A couple of hours later, just as I was dozing in and out of a peculiar dream about goldfish in bowls who couldn't talk to each other, Mum burst into the room like a hurricane, arms waving all over the place.

'Jan!' she shrieked – she doesn't very often shriek but when she does it can be quite alarming – 'Look what's arrived for you!'

I half opened one eye, and then wondered if this was just another part of the goldfish dream. She was standing there, practically dwarfed by a huge bouquet of flowers all done up in cellophane and ribbons.

'James rang earlier,' she beamed. 'I told him you weren't very well. Then a minute ago these arrived for you. Read the card!'

She handed it to me and I gazed at it blearily.

'Flowers for a wet day. Get better soon. Love, James'.

Maybe summer colds always make you want to throw up, or maybe I'm allergic to cellophane and pretty cards, but I felt distinctly queasy.

'I'll go and arrange them.' Another beam. 'Oh, that Tim Dawson person rang. He asked', beams had given way to frowns, 'if you could ring him back as soon as possible. He apparently has something important he wants to talk about.'

Almost before she'd finished the sentence I was throwing on my dressing gown and clattering downstairs.

'Tim?' I said shakily into the receiver, aware of Mum marching past, flowers aloft.

'No, dear, it's his mother,' a warmly comforting voice answered. 'Hold on. I'll get him for you. Is that Jan by any chance?'

'Y-yes,' I stuttered and sneezed at the same time.

'He won't be a second, and I'm sorry about your cold, dear. Summer colds are awful. They seem to go on for ever. Whenever I get one I just want to curl up and die. But the funny thing is,' she continued chattily, 'I don't ever seem to remember having one when I was a child. Do you? Of course, the days were always sunnier and longer then, or that's how they seemed.'

I blinked and stared at the phone. Either I was mad, or the world was mad, or I wasn't mad at all and was listening to someone very sane indeed who understood chaotic confusion and wasn't in the least bothered by it.

'Here's Tim now, Jan,' the voice smiled. 'Do come and see us some time, won't you?'

'Y-yes,' I stuttered again as Mum marched back past with the best cut-glass vase full of flowers.

'Hi, love,' Tim said easily, and I felt a bit of the tension in my shoulders begin melting. 'Listen, I've got some bad news. Sorry to get you out of bed and all that – I'd've sent a grape if I'd known – but H has disappeared.'

'H has *what*?' I don't very often shriek either, and shrieking with a cold can be very painful on the vocal chords.

'Gone off. Done a runner. Vanished. Apparently into thin air.' Despite the fact he was trying to keep his voice light I suddenly realized how worried he was. 'She packed some things in her sports grip, took her TSB savings book, left a note for her mother with no forwarding address but apparently apologizing for breathing – and went while her mum was out getting some fish. The poor woman's going round the bend, wants to call in the police and everything but I said to wait until I talked to you first.'

I stifled a sneeze, closed my eyes and sighed. H was really turning into a thorough pain with all these disappearing, thinking acts.

'Got any ideas?' Tim asked, far too brightly this time.

'Slow strangulation or a ball and chain,' I coughed. 'Does Paul know?'

'I haven't been able to get hold of him so far. Somebody said they thought he'd gone into Hastings. And anyway when he finds out he'll probably only have a nervous breakdown.'

'He won't be the only one,' I muttered, then tried to force my muzzy head to think sensibly. H could be literally anywhere, from Ashford to Australia – well, not quite Australia already, but I wouldn't put it past her to try it.

'I'll go and get dressed,' I said wearily. 'If your motor vehicle really is working you'd better bring it round and we'll go on a magical mystery tour. See you in a bit.' Then I put the receiver down and plodded upstairs.

I looked longingly at what had been my nice warm bed, then sat down on the edge of it and had my usual fight trying to get into my knickers and tights.

I ached from head to toe. My nose felt the size of a house, and by the time I'd finished struggling with my hooded sweatshirt I felt not only cross, but downright put upon.

'And just where', Mum didn't exactly have her hands on her hips, but the impression was much the same, 'do you think you're going? An hour ago you thought you were dying. Isn't this a somewhat miraculous recovery?'

'I still am dying.' This time it was my trainers that'd decided to fight me. 'But H has apparently decided to disappear and Tim and I are going to look for her.'

'What about James? What do I tell him when he comes round to see you?'

'I didn't know James *was* coming round to see me! Why is James coming round to see me? Who invited him, because I certainly didn't!'

She got terribly busy with a duster and a tin of Pledge and at least looked suitably flustered.

'I just mentioned when he rang you were under the weather and perhaps a little visit from him would cheer you up. He's a very nice boy, exactly the sort of boy I'd like to see you going around with.'

'*Mum!*' I exploded. 'Will you kindly stop this sudden severe attack of matchmaking? James probably is a very nice boy but I don't think he's my type of very nice boy, so just leave it out, will you? I'm old enough and ugly enough' – and I certainly felt it – 'to find somebody for myself!'

'But you *did* find him, dear,' she said reasonably, which fact I couldn't deny so I shrugged and mumbled, 'Yes, but that was an accident.'

'So what do I tell him?' The polishing activities were getting more and more furious.

'Oh tell him – tell him to go and boil his head, or chase a haggis or something! I don't care! I want to find H and find out what the heck she thinks she's playing at and I don't feel well – and that'll be Tim at the door now. I'll see you later.' Then before I could get any more maternal advice of whatever description I snatched up my bag and my anorak and ran.

Tim was standing on the pavement and I almost went straight past him.

'Hey!' He grabbed my arm. 'What's going on? The car's up that way, and a very nasty traffic warden was giving it a very nasty look, so don't let's complicate the issue by running in the wrong direction!'

'Oh Tim, I'm sorry.' I let him gently slow me down and turn me round. 'I feel lousy and Mum was getting on my nerves, that's all.'

'Well,' he held open the door of this battered old banger for me and sort of tucked me inside, 'mothers do from time to time, and I'm sorry you're not well but H's poor Mum is climbing walls.' The car engine finally caught and we moved out into the one-way system. 'But what's the matter with H anyway?'

'She's having another funny five minutes. She's about as reliable as a snowflake in a heatwave and if she'd think before she jumped,' I tried to answer, mixing my metaphors or whatever it is you do, 'she wouldn't get into all these hassles.'

'But where's she jumped? Or rather, what's she done?' He glanced sideways at me.

'It all hinges round her dad and the fact the he's apparently coming back, thanks to H, but her mum's got a new bloke, and if all that isn't the potential for a right H-mess I don't know what is! So she's had an attack of the panics and decided she doesn't want to be around to face whatever music starts playing.'

He sighed, and I couldn't blame him. 'It's beyond me! Is she always like this?'

'Yes, she is. And it's beyond me, too.' I sneezed. 'She gets these attacks when she thinks she ought to save the world and when she does you can guarantee there's going to be some kind of disaster. Plagues of locusts aren't in it!'

'Locusts?' He glanced at me again worriedly. 'Jan, you appear to be delirious. Maybe I should just take you home again.'

'Oh don't be an idiot!' I sneezed again. 'It's just a fancy way of saying with usually the best will in the world she gets it all wrong and causes chaos. I learned about the locusts at Sunday School.' I snuffled into a tissue. Sunday School suddenly seemed a long time away.

'Oh.' He concentrated on driving, then quietly said, 'Do we just keep going round and round Rye in circles or have you anywhere specific you'd like to try?'

'Camber!' It came like a bolt out of the blue and I suddenly brightened.

'Camber? Where your Scottish hero hails from?'

'Oh, never mind him!' If I was right the jigsaw was beginning to fit together. H would realize somebody would get in touch with me after the note had been found, and she'd assume I'd go off looking for her on the marsh across to Winchelsea, so I was fairly certain – H being H – she'd have headed in entirely the opposite direction. Over the years I've learned to put up with the utter predictability of her devious mind, and Camber – apart from having James – has an abundance of caravans and holiday homes if she wanted to hole up for a few days.

'Camber it is then.' Tim negotiated the stupid roundabout on to the Camber road, while I sat and H-spotted.

'Your mum sounded nice on the phone,' I said shyly, more by way of conversation than anything else. Now I was really on my own with him in that enclosed space I felt unaccountably nervous.

'She's OK,' he answered in the kind of voice that made me wonder if he was nervous too. 'She's going up to London to see her agent next week. I said I'd drive her. Want to tag along for the day? Assuming, that is,' he grinned at me quickly and mischievously, 'we find H and you live that long.'

'Oh, well,' I was so taken aback at the invitation I had another quick sneeze, 'I'll have to think about it. I don't really know London very well. The only times I've been there have been on school outings, and you know what they're like.'

'I can always hold your hand and lead you across the busy streets,' he laughed, and I decided it was a nice open laugh, not like James's at all. 'It might be a giggle. She's got to be there for lunch and these lunches can go on all afternoon. Just let me know. There's plenty of room in the car. Oh,' he added hastily, 'not this one. We do own something vaguely respectable that doesn't clunk and burp along. Think about it.'

'Yes.' I leaned back in my seat and closed my eyes briefly, partly because I had a headache and partly because I was feeling confused again. 'Yes,' I repeated. 'I'll think.'

Chapter 12

The sea mist was thicker and the rain heavier as we turned into the car park at Camber Sands. Considering it was supposed to be the height of the season there didn't seem to be a lot of traffic around; just a few bedraggled campers with steamed-up windows where people were presumably eating their lunches and wondering why they hadn't booked a fortnight in Spain.

'You stay here,' I ordered Tim as he started to get out. 'And if you hear any loud screams don't call the police immediately. Give me time to swim the Channel first because I don't know what they do to you for premeditated murder.'

'You realize you'll probably get pneumonia?' he asked cheerfully, then pulled a Mars Bar out of the glove compartment and started unwrapping it.

As I eased myself on to the sandy turf which was more sand than turf, a wind, which had nothing whatsoever to do with summer and bikinis, flung itself over the top of the high dunes, picked up the sand and sent it billowing in peculiar shapes and directions. The sky was grey. The tall spiky dune grasses whipped back and forward, and as I ploughed up the steep sand path I could feel the mixture of rain and salt spray being blown in off the sea.

I was playing a hunch, I admitted, wondering if I were madder than H.

When we were little kids one or other of our mothers would bring us here, and when we stopped being quite so little we started to come on our own in the holidays. We never caught the bus. We plodded down the road, past the school, then usually tried to trespass along the back of the golf course when nobody was looking.

We never liked it that much in the summer when the tourists were around and dogs and children were screaming all over the place. We'd got to the sophisticated stage where we didn't mind dogs but naked two-year-olds were a complete turn-off, and large ladies wearing floral dresses or a lot less than was decent, and roasting themselves boiled lobster colour was just ugh-hy.

We had our own place up on the dunes, long before you got to the amusement arcades and hamburger guys and we used to bury ourselves into it and wish the world away until the tourists went back to Pontins and the tide went out into the distance so you didn't think you could possibly walk that far.

Autumn and winter were the best times, when you had the beaches to yourselves and you could walk across them with the wind and spray in your face, then climb the pebble banks and get on to the walls. These were the walks where you could look behind you and see Rye, like a fairytale town high on top of its cliff. H used to say it was better to look at it that way than actually have to live in it, but I never agreed with her and she told me I was a soppy old thing with too much imagination.

But whenever either of us was really cheesed off we'd arrange to go there, and somehow – if it was empty and you could manage to ignore all the touristy bits – it was peaceful. Maybe it was the sea, or the sea and the sands meeting the sky, but it gave you back a part of yourself. And my current hunch was that, even if she was doing a fair imitation of the Mad Hatter, H was looking for herself.

Unfortunately, I grumbled inwardly, *I* was the one looking for her while Tim pigged himself on Mars Bars. *I* was the one who would get pneumonia. And I was the one who would very probably throttle her.

I mounted the sand hill, found our old path – which thousands of other people must've found – and slid down it. In all that sand, and particularly when it's blowing around, there's not a lot else you can do except slide.

My trainers filled up with the stuff and I seriously began to contemplate taking them off and getting *double* pneumonia when I saw this small figure hunched on top of one of the breakwaters, watching the tide coming in.

An enormous explosion of relief thundered through me, the way the waves were doing further out. Then an equally enormous explosion of sheer irritation spun me forward in a slip-sliding run.

'Just *what*,' I said as I more or less landed at her feet, 'do you think you're playing at?'

The hunch hunched forward further, and I've known that hunch for years. It means 'I'm lost, I'm lonely, and I'm trying very hard not to cry, so go away and leave me alone please'.

'H!' I sneezed, and both sounds got torn away on the wind. 'I am your best friend and I have got off my death bed to bash your silly head in!'

'You've got a cold,' she snuffled into her jacket.

'I *know* I've got a cold! I also have Tim making

himself sick eating Mars Bars in the car park, and your mother is having assorted coloured fits. *My* mother is having assorted coloured fits, and you know what that means.' She gave an imitation of a giggle. 'Now before I perish in front of your very eyes and you have to give me a Viking burial or something, will you please tell me what all this is about? I didn't bring Tim out here with me because,' I faltered, 'I thought you wouldn't want me to. I thought you might have some things you wanted to get off your chest which might be for my ears only.'

She hunched again, and I touched her gently on the arm. 'What *is* it, H?'

'Everything!' The hunch turned into a shrug. 'Paul doesn't love me anymore. I've messed things up for Mum if she really wants this new bloke and Dad is going to come back – which means I've messed things up for him, too. You've got your James *and* Tim, only you can't seem to see *him*. The scheme for making money isn't working, so we'll never get to Scotland. And nobody seems to understand me!'

'Oh H!' I didn't know whether to put my arms round her, be exasperated, or just laugh. In the end I simply sat there. 'I never wanted to go to Scotland in the first place. That was all your idea. And after seeing one of Scotland's products, whom I agree you were right about, I don't think I ever *do* want to go there. I don't think I'd be strong enough for all that haggis-bashing.

'I,' I hesitated, 'I can't tell you about Tim. Half the time he makes me mad. Half the time I think he's OK. And if you could have three halves, then the third half just confuses me. He's asked me to go to London for a day with him next week.' I thought I'd better get that out in the open as soon as possible before we had another uncalled-for drama. 'I think I might. It'd make a change,' I added lamely. 'But why doesn't Paul love you any more? That's all a bit sudden, isn't it?'

'He says I'm silly and stupid and frivolous.' There was a hiccup. 'He says I should think before I do things like park ponies in people's gardens.' I agreed with that one. 'He says I don't love him and that what I'm really looking for is someone like James because he's not good enough for me. But I *do* love him, Jan. At least, I think I do.'

My patience was being severely dampened by the rain. 'Have you', I managed to get out, 'actually told him that?'

'Not recently.' She shook her head and a soggy strand of hair flew round in my direction. I had a rather feverish impulse to grab it, tie it to the back of something and then throw lumps of Plasticine at her.

'Well wouldn't it', I took a deep breath, 'be an *awfully* good idea if you did? I mean, if he's thinking one thing and you're thinking another and neither of you is talking to the other then I'm not surprised you can't make head or tail of each other. Who could?'

'Uhmm.' Consideringly, which was an improving sign.

'Now about your mum and all this. You'll *have* to tell her the truth, H. Put yourself in her shoes. How's she going to feel when what she thought was her ex-husband turns up on the doorstep asking to be let in? It *is* because he wants to come back and try again, isn't it? It isn't because he's suddenly asking for a divorce, or half the house, or custody of you – though somebody should have – is it?'

'He wants to come back.' There was an imperceptible nod. 'At least, he wants to try to come back. But Mum seems over the moon with her new man, and I don't want to hurt her. *I don't want to hurt anyone*!' The last sentence had the same kind of nasty wail seagulls develop when they've found a shoal of fish.

'Then stop poking your nose in!' I struggled to my feet. 'Come on. We're going home. Tim'll've eaten all the Mars Bars by now, and I'm probably a stretcher case. We'll speak to your mum. At least, *you'll* speak to your mum. I'll hover in the background and pick up any broken crockery. Then you'll ring Paul, and you'll speak to him, too. And when I'm in intensive care and you come to visit, I don't want flowers, *or* a grape. Something simple like an Amstrad that I can compute you on will do very nicely, thank you.'

A wave lapped threateningly round her feet as I struggled to my own, still hanging on to her.

'Come on, H. Adults are always saying when they tell us to do something that it's for our own good. Well, I'm trying to be adult and tell you this is for *your* own good!'

'Jan,' she turned and shuffled off the damp, rotting timber, 'am I such a fool?'

'Yes,' I said firmly. 'But stop behaving like an even bigger one because I like you anyway. Well,' I had to be honest, 'occasionally. But not when you do something daft and I've got a cold.'

'Jan?' She sounded very, very serious and my stomach sank, wondering what was coming next that I hadn't heard about.

'What?'

'Why've you suddenly gone and got so grown-up?'

I was still laughing as we rolled into the car park and up to Tim's car. So was H, and Tim looked at us as if he wasn't sure he shouldn't be driving towards the nearest loony bin.

'Home, James!' I sneezed, then giggled again, while H apparently had hysterics in the back seat. 'And don't spare the horse power!'

Chapter 13

The home-coming, or going – or whatever it was – was even more dramatic than the disappearance had been.

There was H's mum, my mum, Paul, Paul's aunty Dorothy and a thin little woman in jeans and enormous specs whom I didn't recognize. I wouldn't have been surprised if the mayor had dropped in, or at least a reporter from the free paper.

Everybody, apart from the little woman, was talking at everybody else, nobody was actually talking *to* anybody when we walked in.

'Hello, Mum,' H and Tim said at the same time, and I blinked wondering if I was hearing things or if my temperature had just gone up another couple of points.

'*Harriet*!' Mrs Wyndham-Jones exploded, then promptly jumped up, burst into tears and threw her arms round poor H.

Mum was throwing me 'I-am-going-to-kick-the-cooker' looks.

Aunty Dorothy started bustling around with cups of tea. Paul was giving a fair imitation of a whipped spaniel, and I suddenly realized Tim was leading me gently across the room to the little woman.

'Mum, this is Jan. Jan, meet my mother.' He perched easily on the edge of her chair and put his arm round her. 'And just what,' he grinned affectionately, 'd'you think you're doing here? Or is it another load of background research?'

'Silly boy!' she grinned as affectionately back. 'I happened to bump into Dorothy and Paul when I went to buy some Tipp-Ex.' That came as no surprise to me. Everybody bumps into Dorothy. She's like a news service on legs. 'She told me what had happened and Paul suggested I come round. So I came.

'Nice to meet you, Jan.' She turned and smiled at me this time. 'How's the cold?'

'It's fine. I'm fine. And it's nice to meet you, too,' I stuttered and stammered feeling like a great gawky idiot. Behind her smile Mrs Dawson had a rather frightening assurance about her and you felt – or at least I felt – she wouldn't stand any nonsense from anyone.

'Well,' Mrs Dawson got elegantly to her feet and smoothed down her jeans, 'now the drama seems to be over and the rescue party have returned with the offending object I think I must go and hit George.'

Tim and I knew what she meant, but nobody else in the room did and it stopped the babble of giving-advice-to-H dead.

'George is a very old and dear friend of mine,' Tim's mother said by way of explanation, which was no explanation at all of course, then she reached on tiptoe and kissed her son on the cheek. Neither of them looked in the least embarrassed by it. 'I'll see you later, dear. I think,' she gestured vaguely, 'your father's making beef Stroganoff for supper, so try not to be late. You know how he fusses about when to add the sour cream.' Then with a little pat on the arm and an encouraging smile to me she sailed across the room in her Dr Scholls', had a quick quiet word with Mrs Wyndham-Jones and went out leaving us all gaping, well all of us except Tim that is.

'My mother,' he announced to no one in particular, then gratefully took a cup of tea from aunty Dorothy.

The babble increased in volume and I caught H's eye. She was looking very grateful and trying very hard not to laugh at the same time. At least Mrs Dawson had taken the heat off her for a minute or two which gave her the chance to get her breath back.

'We,' my own mother seemed determined to get in on the act, 'are going home Jane-Anne.'

I gave a mental groan. I could hear the lecture already; how H and I should be more responsible; how I shouldn't be running around with two boys at the same time (when I wasn't actually running around with anybody), and then, just thrown casually in, what on earth did Tim's mother do if she had to go around hitting people called George, and wasn't she an extraordinary lady?

'See you tomorrow, H,' I muttered, realizing with another unfamiliar flash of warmth that Tim was leaving with us. 'And please don't do anything more stupid, like think, it really isn't good for you.

'See you around, Paul.' I tried to gesture vaguely, but it didn't come out like Mrs Dawson's. In fact I nearly knocked a rather disgusting china shepherdess off the mantel shelf.

' 'Bye, Dorothy. 'Bye Mrs Wyndham-Jones.'

Outside the gloomy skies were scudding away to the east and although the wind was still quite strong big patches of blue laced with pink were appearing.

'Have you thought about next week?' Tim said conversationally, and I suddenly discovered he was holding my hand, much to Mum's obvious annoyance. I let him carry on holding it. It was comforting.

'*What* about next week?' I didn't give much for the cooker's chances or Dad's supper that night. 'What are you all hatching now?'

'My mother has to see her agent in London next week, Mrs Braiden. She's a writer,' he explained. I wasn't sure, in the current climate, how that was going to go down, but Mum seemed to perk up. After all, Rye has always had writers all over the place and when *Mapp and Lucia* was being shown on the telly she could never tear herself away from it. She even used to go and watch them filming it.

'But what's that got to do with Jan?' I breathed a sigh of relief. At least I'd got back to being Jan again.

'I'm driving her, because sometimes these lunches can get very boozy, and although she can drive she hates the M25. I'm not too keen on it myself, as a matter of fact.' He beamed. To my complete surprise Mum beamed back. 'I just wondered if Jan would like to come with us for the day.'

Momentarily I wondered if I was being manipulated, but then decided Tim wasn't like that – he wasn't a James – and concentrated instead on wondering what Mum's reaction was going to be.

She beamed again: snow melting in the sunlight. Maybe Tim would be a very good trainee estate agent and sell lots of people lots of houses after all.

'I don't see why not, if she wants to. In fact the change would probably do her good.'

'I'll leave it up to you then, Jan.' He let go of my hand and I suddenly felt lost again. 'I'll be around tomorrow. Go and take your cold back to bed. They say hot lemon and honey does wonders.' Then he walked quickly off to where he'd parked the car, got in, revved up and disappeared with a cheerful wave.

'Well,' Mum looked at me and I could see her face softening — maybe the cooker and the supper were safe after all — 'maybe he's not as bad as I thought, even if he does seem a bit on the scruffy side.'

'Mum, it's holidays. We're all scruffy.' I looked ruefully down at myself and saw just how scruffy I was. 'He starts work soon. He won't be able to be scruffy then. And his mother wasn't, was she, even if she *was* wearing jeans.

'No,' Mum nodded and admitted. 'In fact she seemed a very interesting lady. It's just this hitting George that worries me.'

'George is her *typewriter*!' I laughed. 'Now don't ask me any more because I don't know any more.'

'You know a lot about whatever brought on the H episode,' Mum glanced at me, then shook her head as if she understood I didn't want to talk. 'I'm just glad the girl's safely back, that's all. Now come on. You need a hot bath and a couple of aspirin, and although I may not be up to beef Stroganoff I do still have to stir the stew.'

We walked up the street in a fairly companionable silence, then just as we were passing The Motel she said, 'If you're going to London next week you'll have to buy something else to wear. Why don't Daddy and I give you an advance birthday present then you can go into Hastings and get yourself something?'

I've heard about jaws dropping and now I know what the expression means. Mine nearly hit the pavement outside the greengrocer's.

'But my birthday isn't for months!'

'I know. I said an *advance*.' She marched into the shop to buy some potatoes while I was still recovering. It had already been a strange enough day, and it wasn't exactly showing signs of getting any less so.

Suddenly I smiled. For all I went on about her, for all we disagreed and argued because we both thought we were right when we obviously couldn't possibly be, she was a pretty good mother to have around.

I took the basket from her when she came out and realized, probably consciously for the first time, that she was still young and with her hair all over the place and her jacket flapping in the wind she looked almost girlish.

'I don't want an advance,' I said simply. 'There are plenty of things I can wear, *if* I go.'

'Suit yourself,' she smiled back. Then I froze. Because out of the corner of my eye I could see James coming towards us with that over-expansive look on his face.

Chapter 14

Mum must've sensed me tense because I felt her getting all worried again.

'Just be polite,' she hissed, glancing towards where I was staring. 'He's only a summer person, Jan, whatever he says. If you don't want to see him you don't have to, even if I *still*,' she sounded surprisingly defensive and slightly guilty, 'think he's a nice boy. Still,' she added grudgingly, 'Tim seems to be, too, and if you have to start going around with anybody, which I suppose you will have to sooner or later, at least he and his family are local.'

That particular sentence was going to take some assimilating at a future date, but that date wasn't now because James was growing closer, my heart was sinking and I was beginning to wonder if my cold could take a severe turn for the worse and put me in strict isolation for a month or three.

'*Hel*-lo!'

We'd all drawn abreast and were looking at each other in that way you do when nobody knows quite what to say. James was radiating sunshine. Mum was pushing hair out of her eyes and I was sniffing.

'Hi.' I gave what I hoped was a pathetic little cough.

'She's just going home for a hot bath and bed,' my mother clucked unexpectedly. 'She shouldn't have been out at all.'

'Oh.' James's face drooped a bit like Fred Bassett's. 'I was just on my way round to do my hand-holding sick room number, but I wanted to buy a basket of fruit first.'

'That's very kind of you, James. But I think she would be far better snuggling down and getting some rest.' Mum was firm to the point of being wintry, while I stood there like a juiceless lemon wondering why everything happened to me.

'Ring in a day or two, if you like,' she gave a frosty little smile and I suddenly decided she wasn't nearly as bad as I normally thought, 'but she's probably still at the infectious stage anyhow, and you wouldn't want to catch it and have it ruining your holiday, would you?'

'Ahem yes. I mean – no.' James coughed and backed away a little and I had the feeling if we'd been living in the seventeenth century he'd have been sniffing into a pomander or wafting a lace hankie around to protect himself from the Plague. I stifled a giggle and tried to look extremely ill indeed. 'Well,' he shuffled, 'I hope you feel better soon, Jan. There's still time for us to have another picnic when you do. 'Goodbye, Mrs Braiden. I'm sure you'll take care of her.'

'I'm sure I shall!' Mum glared. 'Now we really must be off. Have a nice day, James.' And without a further word or a backward glance she bustled me up the street towards the Landgate.

'Now,' once we'd rounded the corner she slowed down and gave me an impish smile, 'was that all right? D'you think he got the message that you'd like some peace and quiet?' We stopped just at the top of the steps on Hilder's Cliff that lead down to Fishmarket Road, and she gave me a distinctly mischievous giggle.

'You,' I stared at her and felt like flinging my arms round her in delight, 'are terrific! I've never seen you like that before!'

'I can manage just once in a while,' she said with a smile.

Later, cuddled up under my duvet, with the curtains drawn, a glass of lemon-and-barley and a plate of biscuits on the bedside table, and a copy of one of Mum's magazines on the floor I lay and tried to make sense of it all.

I gave up on H after my first three lines of thought got themselves into such a muddle they resembled Hampton Court Maze.

I pushed Tim to the back of my head because there was something there I didn't have the courage to look at yet, and gradually drifted off into a snuffly sleep. I vaguely remember somebody coming into the room, putting a hot-water bottle at my feet and turning off the light, but bright sunlight darting through a gap in the curtains – and the firm conviction somebody else was in the room – finally woke me.

I levered myself on to my pillows and glanced round blearily.

'Oh, you're not dead then!' H was sitting in a chair reading my magazine. 'We did wonder and I was just planning what to wear to the funeral or will it be a cremation?'

'What,' I brushed hair out of my eyes, 'are *you* doing here? I'd've thought you'd've been under house arrest or something.'

'I said I needed to visit my sick, good friend, and

your mum let me in before she went out to do the shopping. It's nearly lunchtime on the day after yesterday,' she added confusingly. 'And I wondered if there was anything you wanted. Tim,' she suddenly gave a secretive wink, 'sends his love and says he'll ring you later about going to tea. Paul sends his regards and gave me this for you.' She held out a grubby-looking envelope which, when I opened it, contained one of those hearts-and-flowers cards and the message:

> I HEAR YOU'RE SICK
> WHICH MAKES ME SAD
> I HOPE IT ISN'T VERY BAD
> WE ALL WILL SING A MERRY TUNE
> TO HELP YOU GET WELL REALLY SOON.

It was signed 'Paul' with two XXs and I blinked at it again, more than ever convinced the world was a mad, mad place.

'So,' I said eventually, 'you and he are back together again?'

'Oh yes.' She waved an airy hand. 'He apologized for all the things he said and told me he'd never been as frightened as when he discovered I'd disappeared. I think,' she looked down at her knees, suddenly shame-faced, 'he meant it as well. I shouldn't be as rotten to him as I am sometimes, should I, Jan?'

'No,' I answered bluntly, swung myself out of the bed and reached for my dressing gown which H helpfully handed to me, only she wasn't watching what she was doing and neither was I so the dressing gown wound up in a heap on the floor.

'I shouldn't be rotten to you, either.' This time she picked the thing up and did manage to hand it to me.

'Why change the habit of a lifetime?' I grunted, wondering why my legs felt like jelly.

'I saw James.' She changed the subject quickly as if two half-apologies in one day were two too many. 'He was taking photographs in Mermaid Street.'

'He would!' Mermaid Street is one of our most picturesque streets and just about every tourist takes photographs of it.

'*And* he had a little fat blonde giggling up at him,' she added maliciously.

'Good!' I struggled into my jeans. 'A little fat blonde who adores him is probably precisely what James needs. They can run away back to Scotland together and stop off at Gretna Green for a quick leap over the anvil, or whatever it is you do, on the way.'

'I thought you *liked* him,' she said too innocently, and I glared at her, zipping myself up.

'Look,' I brushed my hair viciously, 'we've gone into all this before. I *did* like him, right at the beginning. He sort of bowled me over. He's a perfectly nice bloke, I suppose, but you were right and I was wrong, so can we now just please drop the subject?'

'OK,' she shrugged. 'When're you going to tea with Tim?'

'How do I know?' Sometimes I wanted to strangle her. 'When he or his mother arranges it, I suppose.'

'And are you *really* going up to London with him next week?' She had her I'm-only-little-please-love-me voice on, which normally bodes trouble.

'Yes.' My voice and the decision appeared out of thin air. 'And before you get any ideas, H,' I waggled the brush under her nose, 'you're *not* coming, too! I know you. You'd only jump off the Post Office

Tower or fall in the fountains in Trafalgar Square or something! I'm not being nasty.' I sat down and tried to look at her reassuringly. 'I just want, well,' it was hard to explain, even to myself, 'a day away from here, I guess. *I'd* like to be a tourist for once, if that makes sense?'

' 'Course it does,' she nodded agreeably, then her face darkened and I noticed her lip was trembling. 'Only, d'you think you could be around next Saturday . . . give a bit of moral support? That's when Dad's coming over. I haven't told Mum, yet, but he said he'd write to her anyway. I'm scared, Jan.' She looked it, too. 'I'm terribly scared in case I've gone and messed things up once and for all.'

'Well,' I said uneasily, 'there's nothing you can do about it now, except cross your fingers and hope. But yes, I'll come along and hold your hand if you think it'll do anybody any good.

'You know,' I crossed and opened the bedroom door, 'people are just people, H. And things work out for them or they don't. Whatever happened when your dad went off is really none of your business; it's theirs.

'Come on.' I grinned at her. 'Something'll work out. It may not be how you'd best like it, but it'll work out. Now I'm going to make coffee and some toast, I'm starving. D'you want any?'

She nodded glumly, gave me a lip-trembling smile, and I didn't know whether to feel exasperated or sorry for her. But before I could decide on either the phone started ringing and she gave me a little push.

'Go on!' The smile had turned into a full-blown grin. 'That'll be Tim. I'll put the kettle on while you two decide on your tea-date.'

For some reason, as I started downstairs, I could feel myself blushing and a little tremor of excitement twitched through me.

Chapter 15

Tea at the Dawson's wasn't like any other tea I've ever come across.

H had been right. It had been Tim on the phone, and despite the fact I could hear her giggling and ear-wigging away behind me trying to find out what was being said, I'd tried to maintain as much dignity as possible – but that can get a bit difficult with a bunged-up nose. Finally we'd arranged he'd pick me up about quarter to four, but once I'd put the receiver down panic hit like the 1987 hurricane.

'What's the matter?' H had asked as I'd taken my coffee from her and tried to stop my hands shaking. 'You're only going to tea, for goodness' sake. That's hardly a state banquet!'

'But I've nothing to wear!' I'd wailed frantically. 'I mean, what *do* you wear to go out to tea? *You* should know! You're the one with all the experience! Or so you keep telling me!'

'I shouldn't've agreed!' I'd realized I'd begun pacing and at the back of my mind vaguely wondered if some of H's habits were infectious. 'They're professional people! I'll have nothing to say to them. They'll think I'm a twit and Tim'll laugh at me and I'll never see him again!' For some reason that had become very, very important.

'You're *not* a twit and Tim *won't* laugh at you,' H retorted sharply. 'And anyway your dad's a professional person. You can't *get* more professional than him and his computers,' she'd pointed out reasonably. 'So pull yourself together and stop acting like a Grade A loony. Let's go upstairs and have a look through your wardrobe.'

Eventually we'd decided on a straight white skirt – because it was summer after all – and a pink top, with white medium-heeled sandals, but by half past three, long after H had gone to cause chaos wherever else she was causing chaos, I'd changed at least a dozen times until Mum had shouted at me in exasperation that I was driving her mad and would I kindly go and put on what I'd had on in the first place.

'You look nice,' Tim said as we walked towards the car.

'Th-thank you.' I was so nervous I dropped my handbag and as we both scrabbled to pick it up again our foreheads bumped together. We crouched there on the pavement staring at each other as if we'd never seen each other before and I thought again how brown and alive his eyes were.

'I thought,' he straightened slowly and helped me to my feet, 'we could go for a wander round the town later on. It's a nice day and it'll be one of those soft evenings. I like it when it's like that and all the tourists have got into their coaches and gone home. You get a feeling of – I don't know, *place* somehow.'

'Yes.' I knew exactly what he meant. When Strand Quay was deserted with just boats bobbing at their moorings and maybe a light breeze clacking their riggings, when a light mist, shot through with the pink and gold of sunset, started creeping in from the marshes and all you could hear were sheep baaing at each other, then there was Tim's feeling of place. The town settled in on itself like an old lady in a favourite armchair and relaxed.

'Well, let's see how it goes.' I realized he was looking at me curiously and I hastily tried to pull myself back to the now of where we were.

'Tim,' I suddenly remembered something just as we reached the car, 'd'you think we could stop at Williams? I'd like to get some flowers for your mum.'

'Sure.' He grinned easily and opened the door for me. 'She'll like that. So will Dad. He'll probably confiscate them to use in a still life!'

When Tim let me into his house I had to pull myself up very sharply from gasping.

The long, wide hallway was stacked from floor to ceiling with books and canvases. Papers tumbled off two antique tables and a ridiculous-looking black and white cat eyed me balefully from a shelf, then jumped down and purred round my legs.

'That's Olympus,' Tim grinned. 'Don't ask me why he's called Olympus. I came home from school when we were in London one day, and there he was on top of the cooker. Mum told me he'd just moved in and later on when Dad found him on top of the pelmet in the lounge he said something about the "creature scaling Olympian Heights". He's been Olympus ever since.'

'Oh.' All that seemed to make perfect sense to Tim but it, plus my surroundings, was leaving me feeling slightly giddy.

'Come on through.' He opened a set of double doors. Olympus marched ahead of us – and suddenly we were in a long, low room with french windows looking out on to a whitewashed courtyard that seemed to blaze with geraniums and marigolds and petunias (and various other plants I couldn't identify) all tumbling together in a glorious jungle of colour.

There were more books everywhere, but at least this time they were on shelves; a chess set sat on a low table, obviously half-way through a game; a music centre purred out unfamiliar classical music, and there were bowls of flowers on every other available surface. Light danced through the windows and I suddenly felt very young and very foolish standing there with my mixed bunch of carnations.

It was a comfortable, lived-in family room, but without meaning to, it had an air of vague sophistication I'd never come across before.

'Sit yourself down. Like a sherry?' Tim crossed to a drinks' table in a corner and without waiting for an answer poured me one as if he intuitively realized I needed something to control my nerves, and also something sensible to do with my hands. Olympus strolled out to the garden with that pompous, I-own-this stroll only cats have.

'I'll just go and tell Mum we're here. Won't be a second. Make yourself at home.' He smiled at me, a warm, welcoming smile as if he were glad to see me there, then I heard him run lightly up some stairs, tap on a door and open it.

I was gazing round me, drinking everything in and thinking how different it was from our own long, low room when a tall, broad-shouldered man with a beard and a paintbrush stuck behind his ear suddenly appeared, walked quickly to the music centre, muttered, 'Can't stand Bartok!' and started rifling through a stack of records. He selected one, put it on the turntable, straightened up – and blinked as he noticed me.

'I — I'm Jan Braiden,' I muttered apologetically, struggling to my feet and getting in a H-twist with the flowers, my glass and my handbag. 'Tim invited me to tea.'

'Ah yes, I believe he did.' The man smiled. 'I'm David Dawson. Tim's father,' he added vaguely, in case I hadn't worked that out for myself. 'Got everything you need? Good. Good. Must get on.' He seized the paintbrush and pulled it away from his ear. 'Got a corner to finish full of samphire. Damn difficult thing to paint, samphire. Damn difficult thing to collect *for* painting, come to that. Why does it have to grow half-way down cliffs? Mmm?'

I hadn't a clue what he was talking about but before I could open my mouth to make any kind of intelligent-sounding comment he'd shambled out yelling, 'Maggie! Where the devil are you, woman? Leave George alone. Your tea party's in the lounge looking lost and Olympus is sunbathing in your lobelias.'

I sat back in the chair, sipped my sherry and wondered if the entire house was mad or if it was only me, but seconds later Mrs Dawson bustled in wearing jeans, a loose shirt and a welcoming smile.

'Jan! How lovely, dear. How's the cold? Tim won't be long with the tea. It's safer to trust him than me when it comes to carrying trays and things. I have a tendency to drop them and you can get through an awful lot of crockery that way.'

She sank into a comfy-looking floppy sofa opposite me and rubbed her eyes. 'George is being an absolute pig today. He won't type at all. You wouldn't happen,' she asked hopefully, 'to have the latest statistics on teenage glue-sniffing to hand, would you?'

'It's not really my scene, I'm afraid Mrs Dawson.'

'No,' she agreed and laughed. 'Now for goodness' sake call me Maggie. Mrs Dawson makes me feel positively ancient and, as I'm supposed to think like a sixteen year old all the time, feeling ancient doesn't do in the slightest! Ah, Tim,' she pulled out a nest of tables like a magician conjuring rabbits out of a hat and helped Tim with the tray he was balancing precariously.

By the end of a couple of hours I felt as if I'd known all the Dawsons for ever and I ached with laughing at some of David's descriptions of a camping holiday they'd all had in Scotland where Maggie Dawson had apparently disappeared down a hole in a hillside without either of the other two noticing and where David had been fishing for trout, caught a tree instead and wound up in the river.

Olympus prowled round us all offering paws in exchange for titbits and when nobody would give him any went off in a huff and sat on top of the television.

'Now about the London trip,' Maggie said as Tim and I finally got up to go, 'you and Tim arrange what you're doing, but *do* come, Jan. We can play Trivial Pursuit in the car, I've got the book somewhere. It'll be fun, and if I can get away from my agent quickly enough we might even do some shopping.' She dropped me a conspiratorial wink. 'I still have my chargecard for Harrods.'

Tim groaned and said in a put-on bored voice, 'If you two are going shopping in Harrods I shall unpark the car and drive home without you, and that's a promise, not a threat!'

Outside, by the gate, I turned to wave to them.

They were standing there, David Dawson towering over his wife — she with her arm partially round his enormous waist.

'Thank you!' I shouted and they shook their heads at me and grinned.

'Thank *you* for coming!' Tim's Dad yelled back. 'Do it again soon. I'd quite like to paint you, I think.'

I blushed at that and scrambled into the car.

'OK?' Tim asked as he pulled away from the verge. 'Not too much of a strain? I know they can be a bit overwhelming sometimes, to an outsider that is, but I'm so used to them I don't notice any more.'

'They're lovely.' I leaned back in the seat, feeling happy and light-headed and as if my entire life were changing.

'Shall I park us somewhere so we can go for a walk? I was right about it being a nice evening.'

I glanced at him. He suddenly looked nervous and he was concentrating very hard on the twists and turns in the road.

'Yes please.' Without thinking I squeezed his arm and we both looked down, amazed, at my hand against the white of his sweatshirt.

'Right,' he murmured in a slightly choked voice and headed the car towards The Salts.

Chapter 16

We parked and managed to get across New Road without being mown down by lunatics coming back from Camber. Some kids were playing on the swings where Tim and I had had that first argument, and as if he guessed what was in my mind he half-turned and grinned at me.

'Come on.' He didn't say anything about James, for which I was very grateful, just took my hand and led me down the path across The Salts. People were playing bowls and a holiday-making family were putting things on the putting-green. 'Let's go along Rock Channel and have a look at the fishing boats.' I simply nodded agreement, happy to be with him and let him take any decisions, happy to feel the warm breeze in my face, hear it rustle the leaves on the chestnut trees and look up to see a mackerel sky tinged with pink and gold. The breeze would turn to wind later, the kind that blew rain and spray through it, probably when the tide turned I guessed. But right at the moment it was a perfect evening. I heard the Quarter Boys on St Mary's chime, but I didn't even bother to check my watch. I just wanted this walk to go on and on for ever.

'I used to come here and watch the boats go out when I was a kid,' I suddenly said, remembering aloud and wrinkling my nose as a strong smell of fish drifted towards us. 'H always said she wanted to stow away and she was forever getting tangled up in the mooring ropes and nets.'

We stood for a moment in companionable silence watching as the tide began to lap slowly up the mud of the Rother, then wandered on until we came to the raised footpath at the back of Bourne's yard.

'I like Rye,' Tim said quietly, turning to look at the houses and the Catholic church perched precariously at the top of South Undercliff. 'I didn't think I would. I was mad at Mum and Dad when they said they were moving here, didn't want to know. But then, well, we came down to have a look round and the place sort of gets to you, doesn't it?'

'But don't you miss London? All the bright lights and things?'

He shook his head and squeezed my hand. 'Nope. In London, no matter how long you live in an area you never really get to know anybody. It's all acquaintances, not friends – like you and H are friends. I feel as if I've started to make proper friends here. People like Paul and,' he hesitated, looking suddenly shy, 'and you – and even the awful H!'

'She isn't that bad!' I tried to sound light-hearted, trying to defuse the sudden underlying seriousness of the moment, although I didn't know what either of us were being serious about. 'In fact,' I laughed as we ran down the tarmac pathway and headed towards The Strand, 'she's *worse* than bad! She's impossible!'

Tim helped me over the low wall and we wandered away from the slipway, looking at the moored boats and smelling the mud and the salt as the tide strengthened and began to flow into the Tillingham. He sat down on a battered clump of sandy grass and pulled me down beside him, then as naturally as if he'd been doing it all his life he put his arm round me.

'I'd like a boat one day,' he said thoughtfully. 'I can't sail, but it's a bit daft not to learn if I'm living here. Something like that,' he pointed towards a sleek white yacht flying the French pennant, 'would suit me down to the ground. I could spirit you away over the high seas,' he gave me a quick hug and I nestled closer to him, 'until we found our own private island full of beautiful and wondrous things, like mermaids. How d'you fancy that?'

'Sounds wonderful. But I'm not sure about the mermaids!' I teased. 'Can't we have a merman or two as well, just to keep me company while you're frolicking with the other lot?'

He tweaked my nose, grinned, and for a moment I wondered if he was going to kiss me, but instead he turned away and looked up towards the lock.

'Oh-oh!' His face had darkened. 'Here comes your over-active Romeo. And I don't think there's any possible way we can miss him.'

I groaned aloud. Trust James to erupt out of nowhere.

'It's OK, Jan.' Tim's arm was reassuringly still around me. 'He's got a small fat blonde with him and he's looking very pleased with himself. Maybe you've been cast away in exchange for better things. Though,' he sounded doubtful, 'they're not what *I'd* call better! Now please,' he was grinning mischievously, sending me up, somehow realizing how much I *didn't* want to see James because of the mistake I'd made in more or less picking him up in the first place, 'don't throw yourself at his feet and weep all over his trainers asking for forgiveness. It'll only make the grass wet!'

'I'll throw myself all over you in a minute Timothy Dawson, if you're not careful,' I threatened, grateful to him for managing to be flippant.

'Promises! Promises!' He momentarily took his arm from my shoulders and held up both hands in a mock despair gesture. Then just as James and the blonde approached the arm slipped back into place and I felt him hug me tightly.

'Hi, James.' It was Tim who spoke first. 'What brings you here on such a balmy evening?'

I stifled a giggle. Balmy wasn't in it!

'*Hello* Tim – Jan. How nice to see you.' James wore his charmer smile, the one that didn't touch his eyes. 'I was just showing Gloria the sights of Rye, not that that takes very long of course,' he laughed deprecatingly. 'Gloria, these are some local people I met when I first came down. At least Jan's local. Tim's a comparative newcomer, but he seems to get around quite quickly.' I felt Tim tense and I finally made myself look up at the couple more or less standing over us.

Gloria! Of course James would have to have a Gloria. He wasn't really adventurous enough for a Samantha, and a plain old Mary or Anne would've been beneath him.

'You can't imagine what a coincidence it's been, meeting with Gloria here!' She simpered at him and I heard Tim give a quiet snort. 'She's on holiday at the caravan site, too, but that's never the coincidence.'

'Well, no, a lot of people have holidays on caravan sites,' Tim murmured, and I held back another giggle.

'That wasn't what I was meaning, Tim. No, Gloria

is only going to start at the same college I'm at next term, and would you believe, she lives just a bus ride away from Perth! Small world, eh?'

Tim and I nodded solemnly while James smiled his vacuous smile and Gloria went right on simpering.

'Well,' Tim got to his feet and hauled me to mine, 'we mustn't keep you. I hope you have a good holiday, Gloria.' He gave a little bow. 'I'm sure James'll look after you. Don't do anything we wouldn't.' Then hanging on to my hand firmly he headed back towards the wall, swung me over it, and we crossed quickly towards the steps at Watchbell Street.

I glanced over my shoulder. James and Gloria were standing close together. She was looking at him like an adoring puppy, while he appeared to be explaining the Law of the Sea or something equally enthralling to her. I turned back to Tim, to find him draped over a litter bin in hysterics of laughter.

'Oh my God!' he spluttered. 'Now I think I've heard and seen everything! Come on, Jan. Let's go somewhere sane. 'Small world, eh?' ' he imitated James's Scottish accent. 'That poor kid has no idea what she's let herself in for!'

'No,' I agreed, feeling serious. 'But at least it gets him off my back. Maybe I can actually walk round the town now without feeling I should put on a disguise, or pick up the phone without panicking. It was all my own fault, of course. And it was all because of you. But,' I shuddered, remembering the *They that go down to the sea in ships* episode, 'there's something about him that seems just a little bit unbalanced. I don't mean *mad*,' I added hastily as we went down the steps into the Gun Garden. 'In fact if I'm honest I don't know what I *do* mean, but I didn't like it. It was too – too,' I searched for the word, 'claustrophobic.'

'Well, it looks as if it's over.' Tim pulled me gently into his arms and this time he did kiss me – a light, almost shy kiss, as if he expected me suddenly to pull away and slap his face. I didn't. And when it was over I stayed where I was with my eyes closed and my head against his shoulder.

'What're you doing on Saturday?' he asked, gently stroking my hair.

'Nothing. Why?' I could feel his shoulder-blades under my hands and a quick sort of excitement shivered through me.

'I thought we might go into Hastings. See a movie. Have a pizza. What d'you think?'

'That'd be ...' Then suddenly I remembered. 'Oh Tim,' I wailed, 'I *can't*! I promised H I'd be with her on Saturday and I can't back out now.' Tears of disappointment seemed to be threatening to choke me, and I cursed H for playing games with other people's lives, even if she did always do it with the best of intentions.

'Never mind,' he said quietly. 'Some other time. Anyway, we'll have our day in London next week, won't we?'

'Yes!' I brightened up a bit at that, but it suddenly seemed a long time away.

'Come on then.' He took my hand and we stood for a moment, watching the sun being wrestled down by the clouds somewhere behind Udimore. Out on the marsh a dog barked, sheep called to each other, and the lighthouse at Dungeness winked conspiratorially.

'*Small world, eh?*' The words echoed in my head.

It *was* a small world, and this was my small part of it. It was where I belonged, and no matter what happened in the future I knew I'd always come back to it. The only thing I didn't dare hope for was that, at last, I'd perhaps found someone to belong with in it. Then I mentally shook my head at myself for being so fanciful and with Tim beside me started down the steep steps that run past The Wipers to Fishmarket Road.

Chapter 17

The rest of the week limped to the weekend. I only saw Tim twice. Apparently he was spending most of his time under the bonnet of the family car, making sure it would get us all to London safely.

H was in a strangely subdued mood, although she did manage a row with Paul at least once, but he and I just shook our heads at each other and muttered the normal reassurances about her being back and getting over it. Next day I saw them up the town twined round each other like human octopuses – or pi – and grinned to myself. Paul either had to be mentally retarded, the most easy-going bloke in the world – or one of the nicest, because whatever flak H threw at him when she was in one of her moods he just seemed to let it whistle on by.

I was sitting watching the TV news on Friday night and wincing as Mum complained bitterly at the cooker when the front door bell pealed as if it were an emergency fire alarm.

'For goodness' sake, Jan,' Mum erupted, covered in flour, from the kitchen, 'don't just sit there, answer that!' Obviously tonight's recipe wasn't being the success she'd hoped, otherwise she'd've noticed I was already half-way down the hall.

H was standing there, looking very small and white-faced.

'What on earth's the matter with you? Been down

Turkey Cock Lane and seen the ghost or something?' (Everybody else in Rye, apparently, except me has seen that particular ghost who's a monk who got buried alive for falling in love, or so the story goes.)

'I need to talk to you.' Her teeth weren't exactly chattering, but it was close, so I opened the door wider.

'No,' she shook her head vehemently. 'Not here. Can you get out for a bit. We'll go to the usual place.'

I eyed her suspiciously. Either something really was far wrong, or she was doing her Sarah Bernhardt number again.

'Hang on.' I hurried back to the kitchen.

'What time's supper, Mum?' I was getting ready to duck in case the pie plate she was holding suddenly sailed in my direction.

'When your father gets home. And he'll be in at 8.25 *if* British Rail manage it. Why?'

'It's H at the door. She wondered if I'd like to go for a walk.' I decided discretion and a certain amount of grovelling were going to be the better part of valour. 'May I?'

'I suppose so. But don't be late. Dad and I want to go out this evening.'

'Won't be. I promise. And if you and Dad are going out,' self-sacrifice in the name of peace also seemed like a good idea, 'I'll do all the washing up. OK?' I shouldered my way into my anorak. It might be summer, but there was a chilly mist seeping around and I didn't fancy being frozen. Mum looked at me as if I'd taken leave of my senses, but before she could make a sarcastic remark or start asking awkward questions I hurried out.

H was shifting from foot to foot and seemed to be

counting the cracks in a paving stone as I closed the front door behind me.

'What's happened?'

'Dad's here. I mean, he's here *now*,' she gulped. 'He's staying at The Queen's. He rang this afternoon. Mum was out, thank goodness. But he wants to come round and see her tonight, only she's supposed to be going somewhere with that other bloke and – oh Jan!' She suddenly stopped dead in her tracks and her face crumpled. '*I don't know what to do!*'

'You mean,' I stared at her in astonishment, 'you still haven't told her he's coming?'

She shook her head miserably. 'I didn't know how to. And then there never seemed a proper time to bring the subject up. And . . .' she howled, 'I wish I were dead!'

Unkindly I concurred with that. We appeared to be at the beginning of a monumental drama and I had visions of Mr Jones and H's mum's new friend fighting a duel on Gibbet's Marsh.

I quickly tried to unscramble my brain, wishing Tim were around to give me some sound help and advice, but with H standing beside me, gulping like an out-of-water goldfish, it was difficult. Finally I took a deep breath, closed my eyes and crossed my fingers.

'What, exactly, did you say to your dad on the phone.?'

'Not a lot.' She was doing a good imitation of the incredible shrinking teenager.

'Did you tell him what you've just told me?'

She shook her head. I sighed, grabbed her by the arm and started heading towards her house. 'Where're we going?' she asked dully.

'To your place. To talk to your mum, before all hell breaks loose and you're forced to emigrate. Come *on*, H! You got everybody into this. Now the least you can do is tell the innocent parties what's going on.'

I've never known H to be exactly what you'd call 'docile' before, but she trotted along beside me as if I had her on a lead and was teaching her to walk to heel.

'If you get out of this one,' I sighed as I pushed open her front gate, 'will you promise me faithfully not to do anybody any good deeds any more?'

She nodded dumbly and I pushed her in front of me and watched as she unlocked the front door.

Mrs Wyndham-Jones was sitting in the lounge, all made-up and obviously ready to go out, and she blinked when she saw us.

'I thought you were meeting Paul, dear,' she smiled at H. 'Or isn't that until later? Hello, Jan. How's your cold? All gone now?'

I nodded and nudged H, who took one step forward then several backward.

'Mum,' she mumbled unintelligibly, 'I've got to tell you something.' Then it all came out in a torrent, about having been in touch with her father ever since he left, about this planned visit, about the fact that he was here in town and very probably on his way round and that he wanted Mrs W-J to consider a reconciliation.

'I thought it'd be all right until you started going out with what's-his-name,' H's voice had a rising note of hysteria in it and I threw her a fierce look. 'And I was only doing what I thought was best. I –

I love you both, you see, and I wanted us to be a family again.

'Oh,' with what looked like an enormous effort she blinked back tears and pulled herself together, 'I know I've always said I didn't care and that I was proud to be a one-parent family. And I was. I was proud of the way you managed, Mum, and I know I wasn't a lot of help most of the time. But I kept remembering how we all used to be, so I . . . I wrote to Dad,' her voice trailed off momentarily, 'and he wrote back. That was the start.'

'But,' Mrs Jones looked distinctly shaken, 'I've never seen any letters come here in your father's handwriting.'

'I know,' H nodded shamefacedly. 'They were sent care of Paul.'

'And you mean all this has been going on for two years?'

'Eighteen months,' she said miserably. 'Just after I started going out with Paul. At first Dad seemed really happy. He'd a new job and everything. Then Laura, that was her name, took off with someone else and he got really depressed.'

'So he thought he'd come crawling home!' Mrs Wyndham-Jones snapped bitterly.

'N-no.' H shook her head. 'Not at all. He was convinced you'd never want to see him again after the way he'd behaved. It was,' she gulped, 'me who suggested maybe you should meet up. That was ages ago. Back at the beginning of the year and Laura had already been away for six months by then. He – he changed his mind, about trying to see you that is, because his firm have promoted him and he's going to be working out of Ashford and he didn't want either of you suddenly to bump into each other in a street somewhere and – oh *Mum*!' she hurled herself at her mother and grabbed the astonished woman round the waist while I sat down in a chair and tried to stop my head reeling. 'I'm *sorry*!' she wailed.

At that precise moment the doorbell gave its sing-song chime and we all froze.

Mrs Wyndham-Jones looked at H. H looked at the floor. I didn't seem to be looking at anything, it was all a blank.

'Jan,' Mrs W-J suddenly said in a shaky voice, 'would you be a dear and answer that? H, go through to the kitchen and make a pot of tea. Then if you and Jan wouldn't mind excusing yourselves for half an hour I'd be immensely grateful.' She stood up, straightened her dress, patted her hair – and looked as nervous and quivery as I felt.

H bolted for the sanctuary of the kitchen and I walked unsteadily along the hall.

Mr Jones was standing there and he looked older and greyer than I'd remembered.

'Hello, Jan. Nice to see you after all this time.' He tried to smile but it wasn't terribly successful. 'As you're here I assume my daughter is, too?'

I nodded and gulped. 'She's just making some tea but we – we've got to go out for half an hour. She,' I fumbled desperately in my brain for a feasible sounding excuse, 'she's helping me decide what to wear next week.' That wasn't *entirely* a lie. She'd been throwing stupid suggestions at me all week. 'I'm going up to London for the day, you see,' I rabbitted on.

Mr Jones nodded as if he understood perfectly and I stepped back to let him into his own house.

He stood looking round for a moment and his face seemed to soften as if the old familiarities were folding in on him.

'Is she . . . Mrs Jones . . . my wife . . . ?'

I nodded towards the open lounge door, muttered something about probably seeing him later, then beat a hasty retreat towards the kitchen as I heard H's mum say quietly, 'Come in, Ken.'

H and I did a lengthy and very silent tour of Rye for the next half hour. She trailed along beside me looking like the end of the world, and every time I thought of something reassuring to say to her a shutter closed in my mind. Finally, when I discovered we'd come full circle and were heading back for the garden gate I managed to get my mouth open and say, 'D'you want me to ring Paul when I get home and tell him you'll see him somewhere later on?'

'Like the morgue, you mean?' she asked dully. 'They're going to kill me. I know they are. And I deserve it! How on earth could I've been so *stupid*? Why did you let me do it, Jan? You could've stopped me!'

'*I* could've stopped you?' Suddenly we were in the middle of one of those familiar wranglings, which at least showed she might be down but she certainly wasn't under. 'How on earth could *I* have stopped you when I didn't even know what you'd started?'

We were still muttering at each other and chucking each other dirty looks as we walked into the hall. Then H stopped. 'I – I can't!' she whispered. 'You'd better!' I hissed back. 'Is that you, H?' Mrs Wyndham-Jones said in what sounded a reasonable tone.

I shoved her towards the lounge then stepped back,

waiting to catch her as she ricocheted back out the door. She stumbled forward, hesitated, looked at me pleadingly, then together we walked into the front room.

Mrs Wyndham-Jones had obviously been crying because her careful make-up was smudged and her eyes had a bleary look. Mr Jones was standing with his back to us looking out at the roses, and for no good reason I suddenly remembered how much he'd loved his garden. But there was no broken crockery and no bloodstains so obviously the reunion had been comparatively calm.

'Are you ... is it ... are things ... well, all right?' H fumbled anxiously.

'Are your father and I getting back together again, is that what you mean?' Mrs Wyndham-Jones asked quietly. H nodded so fiercely I thought her head was going to fly off and in those few seconds I saw something I'd never really seen before. Underneath all the sophisticated bluster, underneath all the hare-brained schemes she got me and other people involved in, underneath the cloak of always being *right* there was somebody just as frightened and confused and insecure as me, and I promised myself I wouldn't shout at her again for at least twenty minutes.

'We don't know yet, H.' Mr Jones turned from the window. 'It's far, far too early to make that kind of decision. There's a lot to talk about. A lot to be straightened out. A lot of apologies to be made and a lot of hard thinking to be done. But,' he crossed to his wife, put his arm round her shoulders and she half-smiled waterily up at him, 'we think we've perhaps made a bit of a start, don't we, love?'

Mrs Wyndham-Jones nodded shyly and behind the near-tears her eyes were shining. 'A start,' she agreed. 'We'll see. But H,' she turned to her daughter and looked at her seriously, 'if you ever do this to your father, me, or anyone else again I will personally put you over my knee and spank you so hard you won't be able to sit down for a week! And don't think I couldn't manage it, because I could! Now for Heaven's sake ring Paul – he's been trying to contact you – and leave us in peace. If you're going out take your key because we', she looked up at her husband again and he smiled back at her protectively, 'are going out for a meal.'

The clock on the bookshelves struck the half-hour and I stared at it in horror.

All might be well that ended in H's household, but if I didn't get home soon *I'd* be the one who wound up in the morgue! Trust H to do it again!

'Excuse me everybody,' I blurted out, 'I've got to dash. Ring you later H. 'Bye Mrs Jones – Mr Jones.' Then I raced for the door, wondering if it was physically possible to do a two-minute mile.

Chapter 18

In fact I didn't ring H. I knew she'd be careering around with Paul somewhere celebrating the fact nobody had assassinated her. I rang Tim instead once I'd done the dishes and Mum and Dad had gone out.

'Is — is that invitation still open for tomorrow night?' I asked shyly and heard a familiar chuckle.

'It sure is, l'il lady,' he answered in a mock Western drawl. 'Now how might I be pleasurin' you? And what,' he became more serious, 'happened to Operation H? Has it been sunk, postponed, abandoned, or has MI5 stuck their oar in?'

I giggled. 'The crisis is over. Or at least,' I crossed my fingers, 'it is temporarily. But you know H. *Anything* could happen.'

'Well,' his voice was soft, 'let's run away together in case it does! I'll pick you up late afternoon, we'll drive into Hastings and take it from there. OK?'

'OK.' I felt warm and excited inside. 'I'll be ready.'

Saturday was a bright, blustery day and the waves crashed over the pebbles on Hastings' front sending the kiddy paddlers screeching away in delight.

In the summer Hastings is just another seaside town with candyfloss and hamburger stalls and souvenir shops practically wherever you look. Out-of-season it's a bit like a dilapidated, genteel old lady who can barely remember the good old days.

We wandered about for a bit. Tim bought me a stick of rock and presented it to me with a bow, so I bought him a lollipop in the shape of a skull and gave it to him with a curtsy. Then we went to an early movie, had a pizza after it and walked comfortably together back to the car.

We'd parked it along by the old buildings where they still repair the fishing nets, and even during the day that place has a ghostly feeling about it. At night, with the moon silvering over the sea, which had turned calm, it was like being thrown back into another century.

We kissed gently, then he suddenly hugged me close and murmured, 'I'm glad I found you, even if you've got the temper of a redhead and are as daft as a brush.'

'I – I'm glad I found you, too,' I said, then I felt him raise my face to his and the kiss that followed seemed to go on for an eternity.

When we separated we were both quivering and Tim looked at me seriously.

'Let's go. Before something happens that shouldn't happen.'

I nodded, understanding completely what he meant and respecting him for saying it.

He kissed me again outside the front door, said he'd ring me in the morning, and I let myself in, hugging my stick of rock and smiling stupidly to myself.

'No need to ask if *you* had a good time!' H's voice came out of the table lamp shadows of the living-room at me and I inwardly groaned. I didn't want to see H right at that moment. I wanted to go to bed, snuggle down and repaint the pictures of the day in my mind.

'It's OK,' she grinned, getting up. 'I'm not stopping. I only came round to give you this for your London trip.' She held out a package. 'And to say thanks for everything. It all seems to be working out OK, thank goodness.

'Well go on then!' she tutted impatiently. 'Open it! You've wanted it for ages and it'll make you feel all sophisticated.'

I undid the wrapping carefully and then gasped. Inside the jeweller's box was a tiny silver locket on a chain. And H was right. I *had* wanted it for ages, but I'd never been able to afford it.

'H! How on earth ... ?' I spluttered, holding it up and admiring it.

'Scottish money,' she shrugged. 'I had a bit saved. But after Young Lochinvar I couldn't see you fancying Scotland and, well, I wouldn't want to go without you, and Paul says he doesn't want me to go anyway, and I owe you a lot for putting up with me – so there you are.' Then abruptly she crossed towards me, brushed her cheek against mine and fled through the front door in a windmill of arms and legs.

I stood where I was for what seemed a very long time, then I walked slowly upstairs. Mum and Dad must've let H in before they went out for their normal Saturday drink, but much as I loved them I just wanted to be on my own.

Life was very, very strange indeed.

Chapter 19

The day in London was a riot. Tim put the car in one of those multi-storey car parks off St Martin's Lane, then he and I went and did the full tourist bit. Trafalgar Square, Nelson's Column, St Paul's, Covent Garden, Oxford Street – you name it, we saw it! And although my feet in unfamiliar high-heeled shoes ached like crazy, I wanted to skip and dance and throw my arms in the air – not because I was in London, but because I had Tim beside me.

We had lunch in a spaghetti house near Leicester Square, went back to Covent Garden and I spent ages dashing in and out of all the little shops buying things for Mum and Dad, and H, of course.

By the time we eventually met up with Mrs Dawson we were both exhausted and we'd laughed so much it hurt.

She insisted on buying us tea in Fortnum's, then dinner in a bistro in Soho and it was coming up to nine o'clock before we started back to Rye.

'Would you like to live in town, Jan?' she asked as Tim tried to find the sign-posts for the M25.

I thought about that for a minute. If Tim was always beside me then – yes, I wouldn't mind. London was big and brassy and alive. But I could see what he'd meant about never getting to know anybody there. Everybody was so busy rushing, and if you lived there you'd be rushing, too. You wouldn't have time to stand and daydream.

'No.' I finally shook my head. 'I'm a little-place girl, I think. Maybe that's not being open-minded enough, who knows — maybe one day I'll *have* to stay in London or somewhere like it but I'll always want to go back to my, well, roots I suppose. I understand our part of the world. It's home,' I added simply, and Mrs Dawson patted me understandingly on the arm.

As we started to go down Rye Hill towards Landgate Square I looked up at the old town perched ridiculously on top of its landlocked cliff. It was like a drawing from a kid's fairytale with the toppling red roofs, the twisty streets and the spire of St Mary's dominating it all, and quite unexpectedly I gave a sigh of sheer pleasure. I'd had my day out and it had brought a lot of things that had been hiding in my mind's shadows into focus.

'Thank you, Mrs Dawson,' I said as we all stood on the pavement outside their house. 'It's been terrific.'

'Good!' she smiled. 'Now come and see us soon. Fix it up, Tim, will you?' Then she bustled inside shouting, 'David! David where are you? I'm home!'

Tim looked at me, smiled and took my hand. 'Let's wander,' he murmured, picking up my carrier bag full of goodies. 'A quick turn round the quay, then home. OK?'

'OK,' I whispered, pressing myself closer against him, all the confusions drifting away in the light mist.

The tide was full and the boats were riding at anchor, dark and mysterious against the water.

We levered ourselves over the low wall on to the

tow-path, then Tim put my carrier bag down and pulled me into his arms, smoothing back my hair and smiling at me in a way he never had before.

'Thank you for today,' he said. 'And thank you for being you. Even if you are a muddled old thing sometimes!'

We were very close and I could see his face clearly in the orange of the street lights.

'I don't suppose I'll ever change.' I leaned my head against his chest. 'I'm glad I found you, Tim. Really glad.'

He tilted my face up and looked at me very seriously, then said, 'Are you? Honestly?'

'Yes.' It was a simple truth.

'Then there's something I have to tell you.'

I froze. My heart sank. My knees trembled and I felt slightly sick. When somebody has to tell somebody things in a voice like that it's normally bad news, and I pulled away from him slightly.

'Wh-what?' A finger of wind shivered through me and seemed to toss round both of us like a storm warning.

'Just this.' He took hold of both my hands. 'I'm probably just as mad as H, but Jan, I love you despite your wobbly tooth.'

I stared at him, not believing I'd heard the words, not believing this was happening – that any of it was real.

Then as he pulled me into his arms and I felt them tighten round me I looked up at him.

'Oh Tim!' My eyes were stupidly swimming with tears at the same time as a delighted gurgle of happiness chased through me. 'I don't know ... I'm not sure yet ... but I love you, I *think*!'

'That's settled then.' He smiled, our lips met, and the entire of Rye seemed to break out in a cascade of golden fireworks.

heartlines

Where true love comes first

Other books in the series for you to enjoy

Jane Pitt
Headlines £1.50

Julie had 'it' – that quality that every photographer dreams of discovering in a model. And Jon was a talented photographer who could transform her from a 17-year-old on the dole to the top cover girl in the business.

Jon was also tall, slim and desperately attractive. *He* wanted to shape Julie into a professional model. *She* wanted only to be swept off her feet and into his arms. But the photographer's rule was 'Don't get involved'. . .

Autumn Always Comes £1.25

Falling in love in the summer can happen to anyone. But in a strange country where you can't even speak the language very well falling in love can be the most confusing thing in the world. Or at least, that's what Juanita found when she came to England for the first time. Her pen pal Sandie's family were so very different from her own – exciting, impulsive and confusing. Especially Barry, Sandie's attractive older brother.

Jane Pitt
Rainbows for Sale £1.25

The day Lucy saw the rainbow her whole life began to change. For a start, she was sixteen at last. She was in love with Tony and her future stretched before her like a bright ribbon. She was happy. Then the rainbow brought Tom Reynolds into her life . . .

Stony limits £1.25

For Australian-born Jodie and English-born Sam it was very simple. They met and fell as much in love as it's possible to do! But the past has a way of rudely interrupting the present. And for Jodie's mother, Sam's father, and Barbara Wright – Jodie's grandmother – history was repeating itself and that must not be allowed to happen.

Only young Pia could see what was happening, and in the end it was Pia who acted as the catalyst for something that very nearly became a tragedy . . .

Jane Butterworth
Born to be Wild £1.99

Jossy had spent all her life in the commune. Secluded from the outside world in the depths of rural Wales, it had become a haven of peace for her family and their friends.

Then Alex arrives, on holiday with his parents. At first, Jossy is repelled by his trendy London ways. But then her feelings for him grow, feelings that threaten to challenge her life, her hopes, and everything she believes in . . .

Jill Young
Valentine Night £1.99

Brighton in winter didn't seem to have much to offer Vanessa. No fun, and no one who really understood her. Until she met Dusty. Attractive, gentle and confident – he's just about everything she could wish for. That, and a date for the Valentine Ball. But Dusty seems to have other plans . . .

Three Summers On £1.25

For three years Nell had depended almost entirely on Mark, her good-looking young social worker. When she found out that he was getting married and moving away, she felt bitter, betrayed and all alone. But during the summer, at a holiday centre for handicapped kids, she realized there were those much worse off than herself. She formed the first important friendship of her life with Marion, and although her romance with Marion's wild, cocky brother Dan came to nothing, there was still Jim to turn to. Suddenly the future looked good . . .

Anthea Cohen
Dangerous Love £1.25

Sandra isn't a dare-devil like her friend Edie, but she longs for the excitement of being with a wild crowd like Dan and his friends. During their quiet 'Sandra nights' she comes to know a different, more sensitive, Dan – yet there are still 'Dan nights' when he wants her to join in the excitement of the crowd and their dangerous schemes . . .

All Pan books are available at your local bookshop or newsagent, or can be ordered direct from the publisher. Indicate the number of copies required and fill in the form below.

Send to: **CS Department, Pan Books Ltd., P.O. Box 40, Basingstoke, Hants. RG21 2YT.**

or phone: 0256 469551 (Ansaphone), quoting title, author and Credit Card number.

Please enclose a remittance* to the value of the cover price plus: 60p for the first book plus 30p per copy for each additional book ordered to a maximum charge of £2.40 to cover postage and packing.

*Payment may be made in sterling by UK personal cheque, postal order, sterling draft or international money order, made payable to Pan Books Ltd.

Alternatively by Barclaycard/Access:

Card No. ☐☐☐☐☐☐☐☐☐☐☐☐☐☐☐☐☐☐☐

Signature:

Applicable only in the UK and Republic of Ireland.

While every effort is made to keep prices low, it is sometimes necessary to increase prices at short notice. Pan Books reserve the right to show on covers and charge new retail prices which may differ from those advertised in the text or elsewhere.

NAME AND ADDRESS IN BLOCK LETTERS PLEASE:

....

Name ————————————————————————

Address ————————————————————————

————————————————————————

————————————————————————

————————————————————————

3/87